HARLEQUIN®
Presents

Summer's here, and to get you in the mood we've got some sizzling reads for you this month!

So relax and enjoy…a scandalous proposal in *Bought for Revenge, Bedded for Pleasure* by Emma Darcy; a virgin bride in *Virgin: Wedded at the Italian's Convenience* by Diana Hamilton; a billionaire's bargain in *The Billionaire's Blackmailed Bride* by Jacqueline Baird; a sexy Spaniard in *Spanish Billionaire, Innocent Wife* by Kate Walker; and an Italian's marriage ultimatum in *The Salvatore Marriage Deal* by Natalie Rivers. And be sure to read *The Greek Tycoon's Baby Bargain*, the first book in Sharon Kendrick's brilliant new duet, GREEK BILLIONAIRES' BRIDES.

Plus, two new authors bring you their dazzling debuts—Natalie Anderson with *His Mistress by Arrangement,* and Anne Oliver with *Marriage at the Millionaire's Command.* Don't miss out!

We'd love to hear what you think about Presents. E-mail us at Presents@hmb.co.uk or join in the discussions at www.iheartpresents.com and www.sensationalromance.blogspot.com, where you'll also find more information about books and authors!

What do you look for in a guy? Charisma. Sex appeal. Confidence. A body to die for. Looks that stand out from the crowd. Well, look no further. In this brand-new collection from Harlequin Promotional Presents, you've just found six guys with all this—and more! And now that they've met the women in these novels, there is one thing on everyone's mind....

NIGHTS *of* PASSION

One night is never enough!

These guys know what they want and how they're going to get it!

Don't miss any of these hot stories, where sparky romance and sizzling passion are guaranteed!

Natalie Anderson

HIS MISTRESS BY ARRANGEMENT

NIGHTS of PASSION

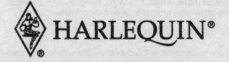

HARLEQUIN®

TORONTO • NEW YORK • LONDON
AMSTERDAM • PARIS • SYDNEY • HAMBURG
STOCKHOLM • ATHENS • TOKYO • MILAN • MADRID
PRAGUE • WARSAW • BUDAPEST • AUCKLAND

ISBN-13: 978-0-373-12737-5
ISBN-10:   0-373-12737-5

HIS MISTRESS BY ARRANGEMENT

First North American Publication 2008.

Previously published in the U.K. under the title
BEDDED BY ARRANGEMENT.

All about the author...
Natalie Anderson

Possibly the only librarian who got told off
herself for talking too much, **NATALIE
ANDERSON** decided writing books might
be more fun than shelving them—and, boy, is
it that. Especially writing romance—it's the
realization of a lifetime dream, kick-started by
many an afternoon spent devouring Grandma's
Mills & Boons® books. She lives in New
Zealand with her husband and four gorgeous-
but-exhausting children. Swing by her Web site,
at www.natalie-anderson.com, anytime—she'd
love to hear from you.

This book would never have been written
without my super support crew:
Mum/Nan, Nanny June, Aunty Margaret, Karla,
Julia and Jude. Thank you.

CHAPTER ONE

EMMA had been frowning at the spreadsheet since six in the morning and now, almost twelve hours later, the glitch still troubled her. And instead of being able to stay on and fix it properly, she had to go and be social with work colleagues she couldn't exactly count as friends.

She stood, stretched, then opened the window, letting the gentle breeze blow the gauzy curtains about her. Fresh air. She breathed deeply.

The conversation from the courtyard below floated up without hindrance. High-pitched female voices that carried far in the still, warm evening.

'Do you think she'll come?'

'She wouldn't know how.'

The women snorted with laughter. Emma recognised them as Becca and Jules.

'Hell, yeah, the woman needs loosening up.'

'I'll say. I don't know what's stronger, her grip on the purse strings or the lock on her knickers.'

She stiffened as waves of cold then hot humiliation flooded through her. They were talking about her. The financial controller for Sanctuary, she was the one with the purse strings. And the lock on her knickers? Ouch. Just because they spoke the truth didn't mean she couldn't feel hurt. There was a lock—of sorts, but more through circumstance than choice. She'd been too busy on her career path. Most of the time she was still too busy to care, but this very second she'd give a lot to change the situation.

They were still talking. And she, foolishly, was still listening.

'I kind of feel sorry for her. All she does is work. Talk about out of balance.'

'Sorry for *her*? I don't. She's a slave-driver. Just because she wants to work like a dog doesn't mean she has to make the rest of us. I want a life, thank you very much. She's only twenty-six and she's hard as.'

Well, that was what you got for eavesdropping. Like reading someone else's diary, you invariably learnt all the things you didn't want to—about yourself.

And now she had to go to the bar to mingle with these women and the rest of the staff of the exclusive hotel who probably all thought the same thing: that she was a workaholic with no life. And wasn't it true? Yes, she worked hard and, yes, she expected others to. That was how she'd been raised. She'd followed her father's rules: you work hard, you get the rewards—the praise, the attention and maybe even the love. So why wasn't she quite as happy as she should be given her career success? The fighter in her charged her weapons, but she had to admit she was a little lacking in ammo.

As quietly as she could she shut the window. She'd heard enough. She wasn't going to let them get to her—much. But she did want to prove them wrong. Was she coming? Hell, yes. Some time. Somehow. She'd go to those drinks and smile and laugh and act interesting even if it killed her.

She checked her perfectly applied lipstick and ensured there was no stray wisp of hair escaping her immaculate French roll. Appearances were everything. And after all, the perfectionist retentive look was what they expected.

She paused on her way out to bend and take in a whiff of the white hyacinth in the single-stem specimen vase that sat on her desk. It was the only personal item to feature in her self-imposed clean-desk policy. A little revived by the fresh scent, she tossed her head high and pretended she didn't care.

Once she was at the bar her resolve fragmented and she gravitated, as usual, to Max as soon as she arrived. In no time at all they were locked in work discussion. Work on the refurbishment of the hotel was due to start tomorrow and there was a myriad of issues surrounding it. A workaholic, Max saw her in the same mould. He'd taken her on as a graduate and through his mentoring she'd rapidly progressed. Working all hours, she'd more than met the challenge. Now he'd sold the hotel to a larger chain specialising in unique boutique hotels—hence the refurbishment. Not far off retirement, Max had taken the opportunity to cash in, but he predicted a glowing future for her. The chain had hotels in several cities and if she played her cards right, she could have her pick of any of them.

Problem was, she didn't know if she wanted to go through with that. Bigger hotel. Bigger hours. And she was beginning to think she might like more of a life. She'd spent all of it so far fulfilling the expectations of others. And she wasn't sure the results were worth it. But she couldn't tell Max that, not when he'd given her such an opportunity, not when he was one of those people she felt compelled to please.

She glanced over to where the other women were grouped— giggling, guzzling lurid-coloured cocktails and flirting with the bar staff. Here she was, still talking shop with the sixty-five-year-old boss and sipping slowly from the dry lemonade in her hand.

Dull, dull, dull. Those women were right. Depression weighed in her stomach. She'd been working so hard—and for what? Whose dream was she chasing?

She excused herself and went to the bar, getting the bartender to add a splash of gin to her glass. Taking a sip, she turned and glanced away from her colleagues and out across the bar. It had yet to really fill up; a few patrons sat at tables and across the way a couple of guys were playing pool. She couldn't help but watch the one currently taking a shot. He had his back to her and was providing a great view of a particularly great butt. Just because she didn't get to play, she could still look and appreciate. His long legs, slightly spread, were clad in denim. His white tee shirt

pulled tight across broad shoulders and muscular back. He held
the pool cue with an easy, practised hand and as he bent over
the table the whole effect of beautiful-bodied male was magnified.

He took the shot and sank it. His mate groaned. One more shot
from the same angle and the game was his. The player rose and
walked around the pool table to collect his drink and that was
when Emma really stared. She knew that face. And well she knew
the cheeky smile that so often graced it.

Jake Rendel.

The depression evaporated and a childlike joy filled her.
She hadn't seen him in years, but he'd always shown her a
friendly face. And a friendly face was the lift she needed right
now.

She forgot the fact that as a teen she'd scarcely been able to
look at him without blushing because she'd had such a crush on
him. She was so pleased to see him that without thinking she
marched straight over, beaming. 'Jake Rendel. How are you?'

The look of shock on his face would have been enough to send
her scuttling back to the corner fast if it hadn't been replaced so
swiftly by the gorgeous smile that had always knocked her pulse
way off kilter. That lock on her knickers rattled.

'Emma Delaney, what a surprise.' His voice was as warm
as his smile.

Her pulse skipped another notch higher. She'd forgotten how
handsome he was. She had another quick sip of her drink and
somehow got the guts to smile back.

She glanced behind him and saw Jules and Becca staring at
her. She seized the ammo. She'd prove she could have a conversation with a gorgeous guy and it not be about work. They didn't
have to know she'd known him all her life. She widened her
smile, looked right back into Jake's eyes and said in the sassiest
way she'd ever attempted, 'It's been far too long.'

He blinked. 'It certainly has. You're all grown-up now.' His
gaze skittered over her. 'And definitely as successful as you
were always going to be. What are you doing here?'

'Work drinks. You?'

'Similar.' His mate seemed to have slunk off leaving them in the corner by the pool table.

There was a pause. Emma struggled to think what to say. Struggled not to stare at him. He'd done some growing up too in the last few years. That fit teenage boy had turned into an even fitter, broader male. Was it possible for a man to be beautiful? If so, Jake Rendel was the definitive example.

The silence was bordering on too long and she became aware he was staring at her as much as she was him. She ran her tongue across her lip, the way his attention was focussed on her mouth, she thought something must be out of place.

Finally Jake elaborated. 'I'm working on a building contract at the hotel nearby for a few weeks.'

'Sanctuary?' she asked, relieved the conversational ball was rolling again.

He nodded.

'I'm the financial controller there.'

He grinned. 'So our paths will be crossing some more. Excellent, you can introduce me round.'

She could. And then stand back and watch as the women queued up. She looked over to where they stood, sorry the fantasy that she'd been flirting with some hot guy would be shattered so soon. He'd be at work tomorrow and they'd know she'd just been talking shop with him tonight.

'You've always stayed in Christchurch?'

She looked back to Jake and answered his conversation-filler question. 'Never left the place. School, then uni, now the job at Sanctuary. It's what I know.'

She'd been packed off to boarding-school from age six. Christchurch was far more her home than the country town where her parents and Jake's mother lived in neighbouring properties.

'You look beautiful—very much the professional city slicker.'

Beautiful? Visions of his old girlfriends leapt into her mind and dampened her smile. She wasn't his kind of beautiful.

'We are what we are, Jake,' she said a little ruefully, wishing her life wasn't all white-collar work. Still smarting from the opinions of her co-workers.

'Well, sometimes we're what we're required to be,' he answered.

She looked at him, disconcerted. The comment was a little close to her own doubting thoughts for comfort. His smile was still easy, but his eyes were astute. She decided to try to keep up the sass, play it light and cool as Jake himself always seemed to. 'You think? What are you required to be, Jake?'

He took a moment to reply and when he did light danced in his eyes and the slow grin revealed his rascal-like humour. 'Well, I can be anything you want me to be, Emma.'

He seemed to have moved nearer, with his body now blocking most of the room from her view, making it feel as if there were no one else there. His voice dropped and she had to lean a little closer herself.

'Is that so?' Her voice had dropped in pitch too. She glanced over to where the others were standing. They were still staring. Glancing back at Jake, she discovered that somehow he'd moved even closer.

'Sure. Anything you'd like. Got any suggestions?'

She couldn't stop the twist to her lips. She could think of a few off the top of her head and not one of them could she utter aloud. Not in this universe. If she were starring in an X-rated movie— maybe. The crush she'd had as a teen came rushing back. She liked him. Always had. Of course, so had the rest of the female population and he'd liked them right back. But not her; he'd only ever been that scamp of a boy living next door who once was a friendly ear that day in the park. Since then she hadn't been able to look at him without turning the colour of an overly ripe tomato. The tomato effect was happening right now, she could feel the heat. Her suggestions? Secret dreams destined to remain silent.

Her silence didn't seem to bother him. 'You know what I'm thinking?' He was looking inspired. 'I'm thinking I should have given you a "hello again" hug. Seeing it's been so long.'

How long had it been? Must be at least eight years. But she was vaguely aware of what he'd been doing in that time. Her sister Lucy was his sister Sienna's best friend. So she knew he wasn't married—chances of that seemed minute. Jake played around. Everyone knew that.

'A hug?' Her attempt at a confident social persona slipped a little.

'Yeah, or maybe even a kiss.'

She tried to look away. She really did. She even managed it for a split-second before she gave up and stared back into those beautiful big blue eyes twinkling at her. Daring her.

'A hello kiss? Just friendly?' She was thinking peck-on-the-cheek friendly, but she wasn't so sure Jake was.

'Sure. Friendly. Maybe we could see how friendly. What do you think?'

Think? How could she think when he seemed to be getting ever closer, his voice lower? Invading her space, spellbinding her. He'd had the reputation for being fast back then. Clearly it was deserved.

She glanced away again, not focussing on the girls that time; she was looking inwards as her heart hammered. Jake Rendel had just asked to kiss her. Maybe today wasn't so bad. Becca's words came back to haunt her—'she wouldn't know how'; 'needs loosening up'; 'hard as'—that was the one that hurt most. The pain pushed her into crossing her own boundaries.

'OK.' Totally breathy, not remotely sassy and not the answer she'd meant at all. She was supposed to have laughed the suggestion off.

Too late. He edged nearer the wall, eyes glittering. The rest of the room disappeared. She stared up at him. One teen dream about to be realised. What would he be like? Hell. What would she be like? Embarrassment overcame her. The heat in her cheeks was at boiling point and her nerve failed. She was no good at this sort of thing, those women were right—she didn't know how and she was about to make a colossal fool of herself. But just as she went to duck away and escape he leaned in, brushing his lips against hers. Ever so gentle, ever so light. She froze. The sensation was soft and warm and she couldn't move away.

He brushed again. Now she didn't *want* to move away. Her lips parted slightly as she breathed and instead of brushing lightly the third time, he lingered. His mouth moved over hers, slow, warm, increasingly insistent. And without thought, without will, she opened to him.

His response was immediate yet still slightly measured, a gentle exploration that teased and tantalised and held the promise of sensual secrets. No other part of their bodies touched. It was as if he knew she felt flighty and he was giving her every opportunity to take off if she wanted to.

She didn't want to.

And inside things really began to happen. As he increased the pressure and depth of his lips and tongue on hers she felt a tingling rise from the depths of her belly to her breast and then it seemed to run through every vein to every part of her body. Like a flower given water she began to blossom, a seductive sensation caused by the six-foot-one pack of gorgeousness in front of her.

Her fingers curled tighter around her glass. And running through her head was the mantra that this was Jake Rendel and he was kissing her. And then even that last thought began to slip away as excitement overwhelmed her. Hesitantly she kissed him back. Then less hesitantly as the taste of him drugged her, made her want more. Hunger. She moaned as she realised the beginnings of a dream. She lifted one hand to his chest. The heat of his body through the cotton tee shirt was as welcome as a roaring fire on the frostiest night. She wanted to get closer to it, uncaring of the risk of burning her fingers. The pressure and depth magnified. His faint stubble teased her soft skin; his masculine scent dizzied her mind. Her body swayed towards his and she only just held her balance.

He lifted his head away. She rocked back on her heels, blinking several times, and saw him studying her expression. Utterly muddled, she tried to look back with what she hoped was cool aplomb. Jake Rendel had been the most popular boy in town and he'd gone through every single one of the beautiful girls that had thrown themselves at him.

He knew what he was about.

She didn't.

He took the glass from her fingers and set it on the table that stood conveniently near. Things always worked that way for Jake. He stepped near enough for her to feel his energy but not close enough that they were actually touching. A sliver of electric-charged atmosphere separated them.

'Going for more than friendly now, Emma,' he warned her.

She didn't reply—was incapable of speech; she thought she'd just had more than friendly. She wasn't sure she could handle the next level of Jake. What had started as a friendly hello was now a situation rapidly slipping out of her control. Jake Rendel in full force and taking no prisoners.

Jake held back to watch as her blurry eyes widened and he inwardly chuckled. Who'd have thought that shy little Emma Delaney would grow up into someone quite like this? Someone who could kiss quite like that? Outwardly uptight, but in action? Not uptight at all. Body-burning. How intriguing. He breathed in to catch her scent: floral, fresh. She looked like a strict school-marm but she smelt of spring.

He'd never really thought about kissing Emma Delaney before, but then he'd never noticed that soft, full mouth before either. Not 'til she'd popped up right in front of him tonight with a sensuous half-smile and smoky eyes.

His five weeks in Christchurch might be more fun than he'd envisaged with her working at the hotel. An interesting possibility. Different.

He was about to investigate further, wanting to kiss her again, when he saw it—another glance over his shoulder. Her glazed look sharpened into deadly accurate focus. He knew for that second her mind was miles away from him.

It was on someone else.

Red alert. Emma Delaney was playing him off. Only interested in seeing someone else's reaction. He shelved plans for a five-week fling and backed off. Stepping away, his smile wiped. This party was over before it had even begun.

He had her attention again but her confused look didn't move him. With a level of discipline that would impress army recruiters, he managed not to spin round and glower at the bloke she was obviously so concerned about. 'Who is it you're watching, Emma? Have you made him jealous?'

'What?'

'Whichever guy it is behind me you're so interested in.'

The shock in her expression had him wondering if he'd just made a huge mistake, but then he saw the flicker of guilt. He'd been right. She was focussed on someone else. Her face coloured instantly.

'I don't like to be used, Emma, and I'd never have picked you for one who played games.'

She opened her mouth and closed it again.

Adrenalin surged through him, making him feel as if he'd powered out on a sea kayak and wrestled with the waves for hours. Instead it had just been a kiss—one that had started out tame enough, but that had ended with him contemplating much more. And he knew she had been too, he'd seen the look in her eye, tasted the hunger in her lush mouth. Had she been honest, he'd have done it again and again. As it was, no, thanks, there were plenty of other fish to fry.

Her skin had yet to return to its normal creamy colour and she was obviously trying to think what to say. He saved her the trouble. 'See you 'round, Emma.' He walked away, leaving her standing there.

Emma watched him rejoin his friend and knew she couldn't leave things like that. He'd gone from devastatingly flirtatious to coldly remote in a blink. He had it partly right but she hadn't been playing him off against some other guy. If she weren't in such a whirl she'd have laughed at the absurdity of that thought. But she was too thrown by the kiss, and she couldn't bear for him to think badly of her.

Sure, she'd acted up initially because the witches had been watching, but within seconds she'd been under his spell just as she'd always been. And amazingly he'd been conjuring it all up for *her*. Not some beautiful bimbo like he'd usually hung with back in the days when their paths had crossed. No, the fact was she couldn't have cared less about anything or anybody once his lips had touched hers. Good grief. This was what she'd been missing?

Then again, she'd always had a thing for Jake. Gut instinct had been so right. And now gut instinct was telling her to come clean to him. She followed him, knowing her face must be completely beetroot. 'Jake, for what it's worth, it wasn't any *guy*.'

He stood silent.

She took a deep breath. 'It was a couple of female workmates. I'd overheard them earlier talking about me. About my, uh, non-existent love life.' She couldn't bear to look at him at that moment and she pressed on, desperate to get over that most awkward bit. 'I admit it was nice to be seen talking to a guy like you and... um...' Stammering and not quite sure where she was heading, she finally dared look into his face. His expression was lighter.

Then he helped her out. 'A guy like me?' He waggled his brows.

'Yeah.' She tossed her head up, her confidence growing. The lift from his kiss bolstered her decision to be honest. 'You know, Jake. Women only take one look at you and know you'll be fun to play with. And now I know why.'

His amused look deepened. 'I *think* that's a compliment.'

She smiled back, relieved he was no longer angry. She wanted to make things better. 'You really do know how to kiss.' Oh, my God. She hadn't meant for that to slip out. She knew her cheeks were really glowing now—and not just her cheeks. An all-over body blush.

'You think so?' He ran his hand over his jaw and the smile that tugged at the corner of his mouth was definitely wicked. He lowered his voice and leaned closer. 'Well, if you want a repeat, you just let me know.'

Impossibly she coloured even more, feeling the blaze in her face. She lifted her hands to block her cheeks from sight. Positively frizzling—hot enough to fry an egg on. He must think she was such an idiot. The world's biggest nerd—earnest Emma caught out at trying to be flirty.

A repeat? Well, that would be just fine if his impact on her weren't quite so overpowering. A playful kiss for him was an earthquake event for her. Quite why she'd thought she'd be able to handle saying yes to Jake Rendel was beyond her. He played around and she'd never been any good at team sports. Too embarrassed and tongue-tied to reply, she turned to leave, but his hand shot out to grip her arm.

'I don't mind playing games, Emma, but the games I play have only two players who both know the rules…' He stepped closer again and, like the rabbit caught by the glare of the headlights, she wasn't able to move.

'Rules?'

He nodded, leaning down to whisper in her ear, his voice low and sexy as hell. 'No audience. No ulterior motives. And…' he paused, and the wicked gleam in his eye flared to a full-blown inferno '…no clothes.'

At his sudden smile she knew he'd heard her soft gasp.

Jake Rendel had always been popular because of his good humour, his easy charm. Popular with women. Beautiful women.

She glanced over to where Becca and the others stood, still staring from behind their drinks. Their less-than-subtle laughter ate at her confidence. She looked back at Jake. He'd followed her line of sight and was smiling at the group of women unashamedly watching them. She saw the assessing sparkle in his eye, the appreciation. And then the reality hit her. If she hadn't come over to him initially, and if she wasn't standing here now telling him about her sub-standard social life he'd be over there working his charm on the whole bunch of blondes.

She was Emma. Geek girl. In no way was she anything like Jake's old girlfriends and, if the attention he was currently bestowing on her co-workers was anything to go by, he didn't appear to have changed too much.

He must have wanted to kiss her out of sheer curiosity. To see if she even *would.*

He looked back at her and his smile widened. Jake was amused. But if he was laughing, he must be laughing *at* her, not with her, because she wasn't laughing at all.

She stepped back as humiliation drowned the last of the delight she'd felt from his touch. She'd been pretending she could flirt and, boy, had she been wrong about that. She couldn't match him. Was hopeless at the whole thing. He'd think she was even more pathetic than when they'd last had a conversation. Jake Rendel messed around. She never did.

She pulled her brain back to business, hiding the fluster. She had a big day on the job tomorrow. She needed to be on top form for that—couldn't let Max down, wouldn't let herself down.

She reverted back to the formal politeness that served her so well. 'Nice to see you again, Jake. Take care.' She knew the platitudes sounded ridiculous after the passionate way she'd just kissed him. She graced him with one of her trademark polite-yet-distanced smiles and left. She didn't look towards her work colleagues at all.

Jake Rendel. The hottest guy she'd ever known and she'd just made a complete fool of herself. He'd never been interested in her. Would never be interested in her. Especially now she'd proved she was the social slow top everybody thought her. She hoped she wouldn't see him again for a long, long time. Except in her dreams.

And then she remembered.

CHAPTER TWO

EMMA arrived at work even earlier than usual—hoping like crazy the builders wouldn't be on the job yet. That Jake wasn't there yet. The fact that he was going to be working in the hotel had gone in one ear and out the other in the excitement of seeing him. Then he'd kissed her—in front of everyone. And she'd humiliated herself—in front of everyone. Especially *him*.

Now Becca and her cohorts would have something different to talk about. Something even more cringe-worthy than her lack of social life: her *disastrous* social life. She didn't want to meet their eyes. And she sure as hell didn't want to see Jake.

Max buzzed her, asking her into a meeting. He greeted her with a wink as she entered the room.

'Emma, I wanted you to be in on this.' He nodded for her to sit. 'You've met Thomas, the boss over at White's Construction.'

Thomas was the same generation as Max. Emma smiled at him as she took her seat.

'I wanted to tell Max in person.' Thomas's smile widened. 'I've handed over the reins. Fresh blood taking over the firm to see it well into the future, just like what's happening here. We've been bought out by a bigger, better company.'

Judging by his pleased expression, Emma knew it was safe to offer congratulations. 'You're retiring?'

'Yes, more time on the golf course coming my way. But this is the man taking over. You have any problems with the builders, you talk to him.' He gestured behind her.

She hadn't realised there was someone else in the room. She turned to see a tall figure leaning against the window and smothered her gasp with a grit of her teeth.

Jake looking totally unlike the Jake she knew of old—the one who hung out in jeans or shorts, and a casual tee shirt. This Jake was in an impeccably tailored charcoal-grey suit. The shirt a bright white, the navy tie classic and understated. Freshly shaved, he looked crisper than she'd ever seen him. He looked like a complete stranger but the imp in his eyes was still there.

Her blush was uncontrollable.

She'd thought he was one of the workers. She hadn't realised he was the boss!

She winced. So much for hoping to avoid him. He'd be in on all the meetings, overseeing the whole damn project.

'You were in the bar last night, weren't you, Jake?' Max filled the gap. Emma glanced at him in horror. His expression was one of wild amusement. 'You already know our Emma here.'

'Yes,' Jake replied, looking at Emma in a way that wasn't reducing the scale of her blush. 'We go way back.'

'Yes, you looked kind of friendly.' Max beamed.

Emma knew her discomfort was obvious and that the Machiavellian streak in Max was loving the whole thing. What Jake made of it, she had no idea. She hoped the whole subtext was going right over Thomas's head. She'd have it out with Max and Jake later. Separately and in private. Wait a second. She didn't want to think about private with Jake. No audience? She didn't want to go anywhere near those three rules. Humiliation territory—she'd had enough of that in the last twenty-four hours.

Instead she chimed in as coolly as she could, 'Actually, we hadn't seen each other in a long time.'

'Oh, well, that explains the warm greeting, then,' Max said with such a benign expression Emma wanted to throttle him. 'Maybe you could show Jake round the place and reacquaint yourselves at the same time. He's only seen the hotel on the plans—take him on a tour now if you like.'

Thus dismissed, she had no choice but to obey. She could hear the chuckles of the two older men as she and Jake left the room.

'Are you embarrassed?' he asked as soon as the door closed behind them.

'No.' Yes. Utterly.

He grinned.

'Where do you want to start?' Focus on the job, not the fit body. Uh-huh. She kept her eyes on the carpet ahead, but secretly concentrated on the peripheral view of him as they walked side by side down the corridor.

'A bedroom's always good.' She heard the teasing lilt.

She had to ignore it. Had to. She was already under his spell and he was *just joking*—knowing she was mortified and turning the screws for a laugh. That kiss had meant nothing to him. 'Let's go to the kitchen area, as that's where you're starting on the refurb.' Brisk, no nonsense, she glanced at him with as much frost as she could muster.

He did his best to look crestfallen.

At that she couldn't help but laugh.

His small smile widened into the full beamer that showcased strong white teeth and emphasised full sensual lips. Her own reaction was unstoppable. The glow inside, the spark of heat, the broad smile back.

'You're impossible, Jake.' Impossible to stay mad at. Impossible not to like. Impossibly dangerous for her.

'I'm sorry about last night if it makes things difficult for you.'

'It doesn't matter. It was my own fault.' The damn blush rose again. She walked quickly, deciding to get the tour over with as soon as possible. 'You saw how much Max was enjoying it. He doesn't mind what goes on so long as the work gets done. I think he quite enjoys "watching the young ones", as he puts it.'

'The "young ones"?' Amazed amusement.

'Oh, you know, bell-boy flirting with the second-chef, waiter falls in love with housemaid. When you've got thirty-odd young staff in hospitality working funny hours, things are bound to happen.' Just not to her.

'Bound to,' he said blandly.

She shot him a look, but retreated when he laughed aloud. She swallowed her pride. 'Look, can we just forget about last night? I'm really sorry and I am really embarrassed.'

'I'm not about to forget it, but we won't talk about it again if you like.'

From the way his attention seemed to have snapped to their surroundings she was fairly sure he was well on the way to forgetting about it.

Right. Great. Determined to forget about it herself, she focussed on showing him the hotel, pointing out the areas where the bulk of the work was to take place. His teasing manner had vanished completely and she was intrigued to see his professional side. She stood back and watched as he inspected the rooms, running an expert eye over the ceiling, smoothing a hand down a hairline crack in the wall. His hands were large and capable and yet he caressed the satin finish with a light finger.

He'd worked wood from an early age—his grandfather had been a carpenter and before he died he'd passed on all his knowledge to Jake in the workshop that overlooked Emma's backyard. She'd known he'd gone into building but hadn't realised he'd taken over a huge firm like White's. She looked at his suit—made to measure. Bad idea, because then she became aware of the body it clothed and the memory of that body so close to hers for those few moments last night. Big. Strong. Heavenly.

He looked up and caught her staring. He smiled, a wickedness stealing into his eyes. She cleared her throat, looked away and led him through to Reception.

They stood looking at the atrium lounge where major alterations were to take place. She was just explaining the rationale when he surprised her by stepping nearer and fixing her with his gaze. She broke off mid-sentence and stared back at him. His wicked look of minutes before had returned full force and intent had come with it. Before she knew what he was doing he slid his fingers through her hair and pressed his lips to her forehead. They stayed, slowly brushing across her skin.

She stood immobile in the light embrace. Confused, but conscious of wanting more. 'Uh, Jake, what are you doing?'

'Cementing your new reputation.'

'What?'

He whispered in her ear, and she tried to concentrate on the words and not the sweet wind of his breath on her temple. 'Is the woman on Reception one of the ones from last night?'

'Yes.'

'Thought so.'

She started to turn to look at Becca, but he stopped her by taking her hand, closing his other arm around her body and guiding her to the elevator, pulling her close as they walked. Trying not to enjoy the entire sensation, she allowed the whole thing to happen.

'She was watching, all bat ears and owl eyes.'

'Jake, it doesn't matter.'

'Yes, it does; it matters to you. They hurt you.'

'Only because I was having a weak moment.' She was having another now, standing with his arm supporting her. If he removed it she just might topple over, yet if he didn't remove it she was going to be in pots of trouble.

'Nothing wrong with weak moments, Emma. Even you're allowed them sometimes.'

The lift doors slid open and he ushered her in. He then proceeded to push every single one of the floor buttons.

She braced her back against the wall. 'Jake, what are you doing?'

'Buying time.' He grinned. 'Not that this will give me much—there are only five floors.' He turned to face her. 'I've got a proposition for you.'

'What sort of proposition?' Business, it had to be business. That didn't stop the acceleration of her heart.

'Sorting out your image.'

Not business. She'd kind of guessed that. 'My image.'

'Yeah, you know, the workaholic spinster thing.'

'Spinster?'

He stepped closer, still grinning wolfishly. 'Come on, let's show them that you're really a foxy man-eater who knows how to keep a man dangling.'

His proximity was making her brain function poorly. The ability for rational decision-making skipped out the window. 'Are you offering to dangle?'

The doors opened on the first floor. Thankfully no one entered and Emma didn't have the will to exit—even though she knew she should.

'Sure, I can dangle real good.' He winked outrageously. 'Come on, I'll be around here for, what, five weeks? Let's give them something new and exciting to talk about. Show them that they had you read all wrong.'

The way he could switch from super-professional to complete clown amazed her.

'I am not going to make out with you in the reception area all day, if that's what you mean.' Was that what he meant? Her heart thudded faster.

'Just a couple of hours?'

'No! Be serious.'

'I am being serious. It'll be a laugh, no harm can come of it.'

She wasn't so sure about that. It might be a fun charade for him, but her hormones were doing silly things and he hadn't even started yet. Have a pretend affair with Jake Rendel? 'Why do you want to do this?'

'I saw the look on that woman's face, Emma. I know what she thinks and she is so wrong. I know the type.'

Jake would. Jake would understand every type and have experience with them all. He clearly read her doubts. 'Come on, it'll be fun. A look here, a touch there. They'll be riveted. You said yourself Max won't care.'

A look? A *touch*? 'What about your rules?'

'Ah. Kissing's different. We don't have to kiss for this.'

Didn't they? She stamped out the spark of disappointment. 'But you kissed me just then.' She could still feel it on her forehead.

'That wasn't a kiss. That was a friendly peck.'

If that was a friendly peck, then she was in big trouble.

'Come on,' he wheedled. 'What are old neighbours for? We help each other out. Let's show them your deep, passionate side, hmm?'

His expression was suddenly one that brooked no compromise. 'You know you want to.'

An electrical charge rippled through her as she saw his determination. He was right. She wanted to, and for all the wrong reasons. She ought to be saying no. She ought to be giving him the kind of polite yet firm brush-off she reserved for the much older, usually married, guests who sometimes asked her out. But some of her just couldn't resist the idea of proving a point to those girls.

She'd always been the hard-working geek. The quiet one who could answer all the questions in class. The only reason a Becca at school would talk to her would be to copy her study notes. The whole men thing came easily to women like Becca. Emma knew a beautiful girl like Becca would net a guy like Jake with a snap of her fingers.

A guy like Jake. And the fact that it was him made the whole silly scheme irresistible. Gorgeous. Fun. Impossible to say no to. She could do this safely, couldn't she?

Wouldn't it be fun to be in on the joke for once, not on the end of it? Despite the nagging feeling that this was going to cause huge problems, the answer just slid out. 'OK.'

Another thrill shot through her as his eyes danced with satisfaction. 'So you can take a challenge, Emma. Maybe we could even work on your wardrobe.'

Her wardrobe? 'What's wrong with my clothes?'

'Nothing.' He was quick to back-pedal. 'They're very…tailored.'

'Tailored.'

He laughed. 'Read uptight-looking. Maybe we could loosen them up a little.'

'I am not going to start wearing sexy clothes at work, Jake.'

'OK.' He raised his hands pacifically before speaking smoothly. 'You don't need clothes to come across sexy, Emma.'

'Have you started already? Because there's no need. There's no one in the lift but us.'

'I speak the truth.'

'You're a silver-tongued devil, Jake Rendel, and I so shouldn't be doing this.'

Amusement shook him. 'Look, we make out like we're having a flaming affair for five weeks and then you crush my heart under your four-inch heels.'

'I don't wear four-inch heels.'

He laughed again. 'I know.'

'Well, anything higher than an inch is impractical and uncomfortable.' Her heart thudded. She shouldn't be taking this from him. He was a tease. He might be a man of experience, but who was he to criticise her clothes? They cost a lot of money. Indignant, she decided to challenge him. 'You think you're enough of an "eligible bachelor" for this?'

His smile broadened. 'You said it yourself, Emma—women like to play with me. What can I say?'

'We can say you've an ego!'

'We can let slip a few more appetising facts if you want, make me more of a catch.'

'Such as?'

'I own my own business with an annual turnover in the millions. I own three properties, including a beachfront home in Abel Tasman National Park that's only accessible by boat or helicopter.'

'Good imagination, Jake!'

He looked at her blandly. 'It's all true. Layabout boy made good, Emma, didn't you know?'

She shook her head. 'Helicopter?'

'With licence.'

'Boat?'

'Three. Sail, speed and a dingy, which is so ancient it shouldn't really count, but it floats so let's say it does.'

She stared at him, unable to believe she didn't know this about him. But then his mother didn't brag quite the way her father did. Eligible bachelor wasn't the word. He should be featured in one of those women's mags. Drop-dead gorgeous, wealthy and funny. 'So why *are* you single, Jake?'

'You said it yourself, Emma. Women like to play, and I like to play along with them.'

Well, at least he was up front.

'This isn't real though, Jake. This is just pretend, *OK*?'

'Sure thing. It'll be a blast.' He leaned against the back wall of the lift next to her, side on, smiling. She felt as if she'd been hit on the head with a mallet and concussion had set in. Was that why she was acting so crazy?

Just pretend. Jake watched her as she slipped back into Max's office. What was he doing? He'd just taken over this company, and had a big contract to fulfil. He was here only for the duration to oversee it and find a new local manager so he could head back to Auckland. Yet here he was setting up a juvenile ploy. But he'd seen the expression of the woman on Reception. She'd given him a come-hither look when he'd arrived with Thomas. He knew she'd recognised him from the night before with Emma and he knew her type all right. The type keen to steal a man from another woman just for the fun of it. She'd see Emma's strait-laced attire and hard-working attitude and miss the hot light underneath.

To be honest *he'd* missed it 'til now. But this time things were going to be different. By the time he was done they'd all see Emma as the sensual temptress he was quite sure she was capable of being. The woman who'd have a man on his knees before coolly discarding him. From the way he'd felt when they'd kissed last night, he knew it wasn't too far-fetched. She packed a powerful punch and he wanted to go for another round. And with a twinge of guilt he recognised that that was the whole point. He wanted to get his hands on her again—test out that seismic reaction. Right off the Richter scale. But her discomfort when they'd met this morning had been obvious to everyone. He wasn't going to get anywhere with her in frozen mode. So he needed to lighten it up. Make it fun—and he was pretty good at that.

He pushed the lift button to ground again and looked to the back of the lift where she'd just been standing. He smiled at the memory of her hazel eyes widening in indignation when he'd teased about her clothes. It surprised him she didn't wear much in the way of heels; most women he knew did—even the really tall ones. A slip of a thing like Emma would usually want the benefit of a few extra inches. He liked it though, liked having to bend to reach her pouty mouth. Liked the fact he could put his hands round her waist and almost touch the tips of his fingers.

Emma Delaney. He hadn't thought about her in years, but there had been nothing else on his mind these last twelve hours. Natural grace, natural beauty, natural talent. And yet she'd always worked like a dog. No matter what she did, the targets she set and achieved were never enough—not for her father. His sister Sienna had talked about the hoops and hurdles Emma and her sister Lucy had tried to leap. Until one day Lucy had simply stopped and Emma had doubled her efforts. As her father had once told him, she was destined for big things and to be in charge of the money in this place at her age was extremely impressive.

There'd been a price, though. How had she phrased it last night? Her 'non-existent love life'. He smiled again at the recollection of her lips clinging to his. He could help her out with that. He really could. Just for a few weeks, have some fun, and give her the confidence and a reputation that would have them flocking. The doors opened and he strode past Reception, flashing a smile of genuine amusement at the blonde behind the counter.

Emma called in to Max to report back. She hoped the colour in her cheeks had died down enough to look less suspicious. Max eyed her speculatively. 'Seems a nice man.'

She decided to play dumb. She couldn't believe she was about to have a conversation with Max about her personal life. Not because they didn't discuss personal things, but because she actually had something of a personal life. 'Jake?'

'Yes. Nice. Successful. Interested.'

'Max, I don't think we should go there.' She sure wasn't. Jake was only interested in having a laugh with her. The whole thing was a joke from start to finish.

He smiled broadly, the twinkle in his eye quite alarming. 'I forget you're young, Emma. You should be wanting to settle down and have a family.'

She sighed. Settling down and family were so far off her agenda and she didn't know if they were ever going to be on it. She was too busy forging this career. And the rest of her time was taken up with her favourite hobby. 'Not in the next few years, Max. I've got a career to build.' She just needed to be sure it was the right one.

He looked at her with his shrewd old eyes. 'You're the most driven person I know, Emma.'

'I'm taking that as a compliment.'

'It's meant as one. I just want you to be sure you're driving yourself in the direction you really want to go.'

She was surprised. She'd never have expected Max to pick up on her doubts. He never seemed to notice much regarding her, except if the numbers weren't going in the direction he liked. 'Max, I've worked hard for this and I want it. Sometimes I get tired, but everybody does.'

'Don't miss out on the fun in life, though, will you, Emma? You can work hard, but you can play hard too.'

She always worked hard; it was the play bit that was new to her. Jake knew how. Her father had commented on it—a talented youth wasting his brain and energy. Emma knew firsthand her father didn't approve of anyone wasting their brain or talent on things he didn't consider were worthy. Clearly Jake knew how to work too—even her dad would have to admit that if he saw him now.

But playing was something Jake excelled at. And, while she couldn't resist joining him in this caper, she couldn't let it affect her professionalism or the quality of her work. Five years ago Max had given her the opportunity of a lifetime. And with his mentoring she'd risen to the challenge and she owed him. 'I'm not going to let you down, Max.'

'I never thought for a moment you were.'

CHAPTER THREE

JAKE strolled back into the hotel having changed into his on-the-job clothes and saw the receptionist trying to catch his eye. She smiled as he headed over.

'You must be the contractor in charge of all the changes.'

He nodded. 'Jake Rendel.'

'Becca.' The smile was wide and inviting, but strangely all he wanted to do was find Emma. With perfect timing she walked out of the office door behind the reception desk. Excellent. Time to put the plan into action.

He smiled directly at her, telling himself the uplift of his heart was from the buzz of the laugh. She blinked, clearly surprised to see him. Surprised and a little cool. He didn't like that so much, and his risen heart lowered a little.

'Jake—' a set smile accompanied it '—I didn't realise you'd be on site so much.' Definitely cool. Too cool for this project. She'd walked around the desk and as she passed him he reached his hand out to touch her arm. She nearly jumped out of her skin and he had to cover the moment with a cough.

'This is the first contract the firm is doing since I've taken over and it's a big one. I want to ensure it's done properly. And it gives me the opportunity to look for a manager while I'm here.'

She wasn't really listening. She was edging away from him, obviously eager to escape. He didn't like it and it was doing nothing for her planned image overhaul.

'You like Christchurch?' Becca piped up.

'Yeah, being here means I get to catch up with old friends,' he answered, giving Emma a meaningful look. It was wasted as she could hardly seem to meet his eye. She'd retreated into a blush again. Not good. He'd liked the hint of sass she'd shown last night and in a couple of her comments in the lift today. It was unexpected, but it wasn't unnatural to her. He had the feeling there was more to be found under the surface. A whole lot more. And he wanted to help her find it. He was doing her a favour, wasn't he?

But he had his work cut out. She was running away.

'Can you have those stats for me by the end of the day?' she asked Becca. The woman bristled but answered in the affirmative.

Jake only got a vague nod and she was off, her slim figure moving as fast as possible away from him. Ignoring the smiles Becca was flashing his way again, he headed in the direction Emma had taken.

Emma hurried to her office, needing some breathing space. The speed with which he worked was frightening—too much. She couldn't go through with it. Not when he unsettled her so easily. She'd nearly had heart failure coming out of the office downstairs and seeing him in the tight tee and jeans that showed off the length and strength of those legs.

She hadn't realised quite the bog she'd got herself into. Hadn't registered that Jake being in charge meant that Jake was going to be on site eighty per cent of the time and she was already overdosing. Their relationship was a charade but her physical reaction was real—sparking.

One minute later the man himself appeared at her doorway. He stepped in and shut the door behind him.

'Emma, this isn't going to work if you freeze up every time I come near you.'

'Jake, this isn't going to work at all. Let's just forget it. The whole idea is dumb.'

'Too late now, the show's on the road. You have to run with it.'

'Jake—'

'You need to relax, that's all,' he overrode her. 'I think we just need some practice.'

'Practice?' What was it about him that had her blankly repeating everything he said? Why wouldn't her brain work as well when he was near?

'Yes, practice. You need to be comfortable with me being near you.'

Comfortable? Oh, sure. When he looked like that the mercury was bursting out of her internal thermometer.

'Let's just start with the basics. Like if I come and stand next to you, don't go ramrod-straight on me, just take it easy.'

Easy? This? He wasn't standing next to her, he was merely millimetres away and she could feel his entire length. Problem was, the nearer he got, the more he felt too far away. So she had to go ramrod-straight to stop from leaning into him and closing the gap completely.

'Take your jacket off.'

'What?'

He sighed. 'Emma, it is twenty-eight degrees out there and just as warm in here and you're all buttoned up like it's the middle of winter. More than that there isn't any skin. We need skin.'

'Skin?' Parrot in action again.

'Contact. Lovers like to make contact, Emma; that's the whole point. No one will believe we're a hot item unless there is some contact going on.' He rolled his eyes. 'Just take it off.'

Wordlessly, slowly, she unbuttoned the black suit jacket. She did take it off sometimes, but only when she was in her office behind her desk. She always wore it when walking through the hotel. It looked professional, and she only had a simple white cami-tee on underneath. That was it—combination underwear and top that she hadn't intended for public display. He stood stock-still, watching as she revealed the front of it. She hesitated, her arms still in the jacket sleeves, as the edges of his mouth lifted into a grin that sent her mercury even higher.

He tilted his chin. 'Off, Emma. Get it off.'

When he spoke like that she wanted to get it on—with him. Practice—that's all. Keep it under control. She let her arms slide out of the sleeves and the jacket hit the floor.

'OK.' He cleared his throat. 'Now, let's get started. I might come up to you, like I did earlier, and run a finger down your arm.' He proceeded to do exactly that. 'No, don't jump and look at me like I'm about to shoot you. You're supposed to welcome my touch, want it, want more.'

Oh. Want more.

She forced herself to stay still, to relax, to think about something mundane.

'Better.' His voice was lower, softer. Way too sexy. His finger slid up again, then traced down the side of her strap, gently nudging it aside to bare her shoulder completely. 'Much better.'

Fascinated, she watched the blue in his eyes darken as he followed the trail of his finger across her collar-bone. Then the fire from that finger hit her and her lungs shorted out. She snatched in a sharp breath.

He jerked his head up and refocussed.

'OK, look at me like you think I'm some really hot guy.'

She was. He was. This was a nightmare.

He dropped his hands from where they were both now stroking her shoulders and sighed. 'Just think of your ultimate fantasy and pretend I'm him, OK?'

Not hard. No pretence necessary. Right now her ultimate fantasy stood right in front of her. And the problem was it *was* a fantasy.

'*That's* better. Keep looking me in the eyes.'

She couldn't look away if she tried. He stopped issuing instructions. She must have been improving. He lifted his hand to frame her face. Just lightly. Then he stroked a finger down the side of her cheek. She wondered if her eyes looked as large as his did. Then her sight was blocked as he lowered his head and replaced his finger with his lips. Gently nuzzling across her forehead. Slowly, teasing down the side of her cheek. She couldn't help but angle her head into his to feel his warm breath across her cheekbone. Couldn't help but turn slightly so his lips moved ever so much closer to her own.

'Uh, Jake.'

It was so easy to close her eyes and imagine it was real. But while his lips were dangerously close to hers they weren't coming closer. Then she remembered his rules. No ulterior motive—not for a kiss. And there was a motive here—practice. Nothing more than a silly flirtation for show. This was meaningless for him, a favour for a friend. And really she wasn't even that.

She clawed back her sanity and reminded herself she was nothing like his girlfriends. A good three inches shorter than the average and brunette, not blonde. And it didn't matter if the bra was ultimate, über, wonder or super, she was never going to be buxom. Hell, if she were completely honest she knew she didn't really need to wear a bra at all—and often didn't, like today.

So, no, he wasn't interested. He was just helping out the 'girl next door' whom he'd never see in a sexual way. Hell, he probably still thought of her as the scrawny kid he'd come across in the park crying that day.

She pushed him away. 'Enough practice, Jake. I think I've got it now.'

He moved back a pace immediately, a faint flush visible on his cheeks. 'Yeah. Right.'

They stared at each other in silence. He stood, hands deep in his pockets, as his gaze flickered over her. She struggled to keep a lid on her ragged breathing. She didn't want him to know how badly he affected her. She needed him to leave now or she'd humiliate herself completely. She aimed for his kind of lightness. 'See you out there on the playing field.'

He was silent a moment longer as he looked her over once more. Then he stepped away. 'Sure.'

As the door closed behind him she shivered. Looking down she saw with embarrassment the clear outline of her nipples. So much for twenty-eight degrees. She picked her jacket up from the floor where she'd let it fall. She was in way over her head—already. How on earth was she to get out of it when such a large part of her simply didn't want to? Living a fantasy. It really shouldn't matter what Becca and the others thought, it really shouldn't. But Jake was right: she'd been hurt. People seemed to see her in 2D—that all there was to her was a hard-working suit. Frozen up inside, and until now she had been. Bitterly she laughed aloud. She was so far from the man-eating temptress Jake envisioned. Then again, wasn't it the bigger the lie, the more likely people were to believe it?

She just had to keep on top of her attraction to him. Had to remember that it was a game. He wasn't touching her because he was interested; it was all fluffy fun for him. But the response *she* felt was real, and somehow she had to keep it in check.

Her phone rang. She picked it up and heard the strains of a twanging guitar. 'Hi, Luce.'

Lucy, her classically trained, country-music-loving, violinist sister, whose best friend happened to be Sienna, Jake's sister. 'What's happening in Wellington?'

The pair of them were completing their honours degrees in Music there this year.

'Exams are over. Now we're unemployed and soon to be homeless.'

'Uh-huh.' Emma couldn't stifle the giggle. She should be strict, but with Lucy it wasn't worth it.

'We're going on a jaunt before the big parental party. Might call in on you. That OK?'

'You know it is. Any time.'

'Sienna says Jake is headed to Christchurch some time soon. You might see him.'

Emma rolled her eyes heavenward. Why hadn't Lucy called the day before? Then she could have been warned and not surprised into doing something crazy like kissing him last night. 'Maybe.'

'Gotta go—Sienna has the engine running already.'

'Don't do anything I wouldn't do.'

The gust of laughter was mildly offensive. 'Sister, you leave me no option.'

The line went dead. Emma put the phone down and stared at it, a small smile on her mouth. Dad had frowned on the friendship between Lucy and Sienna, thought Sienna was a bad influence. If only he knew it was the other way round. When Lucy had slipped off the rails, it had been Sienna who had steered her back on course.

Emma sat and got back to the troublesome spreadsheet of the day before. Only the amount of concentration she could put to it wasn't quite the level she'd achieved yesterday. She smoothed her hair back into its chignon and tried to ignore the flames still flickering at her shoulder where he'd touched her. Tried to stop wondering where in the building he was now, when she was going to see him again, and what he was going to do when she did. And she tried to stop wishing about what he might do if he really were interested and the audience disappeared.

She hid in her office most of the day.

Finally, she had to go and get some papers from Reception—no delaying it any longer. She couldn't progress without them. She went to button up her jacket and suddenly stopped. Skin. She could manage a hint with the suit undone.

'Have you got those stats for me, Becca?'

The grimace on the other woman's face gave her the answer she hadn't wanted.

'I really need them tonight.'

'We've been run off our feet the whole day.'

Emma wasn't interested in excuses. She just wanted the info.

'Becca, I told you I needed it by the end of today.' End of Becca's work day that was; her own had a couple more hours left in it.

'Why not first thing in the morning?' If it weren't for the weight of his arm as he slung it over her shoulder, she'd have hit the ceiling with her startled jump. 'It's not like you're going to be getting much more done tonight.' Jake pulled her closer to him, speaking low and slow, his expression intimate, his eyes dancing.

She would have been very angry if it weren't for the surprise she was in and seeing that shock mirrored on Becca's face. The other woman masked it quickly, but it struck a nerve. She felt unable and unwilling to argue with him—not with the less-than-subtle pressure his fingers were exerting on her tense shoulders. She had to fight the urge to look at his hand as if it were some invading Martian.

'Come on, honey, it's home time. No more tonight, OK? I have other plans.' The way he said it, no one could be left in doubt as to the naughtiness of those plans. How he could get away with being so up front without being sleazy was a mystery to her. Well, she knew how, it was all part of his charm, the teasing, humorous light in his eye that had every woman in a fifty-mile radius smiling with him. Only Emma knew the tease this time was doubly strong. His fingers had stopped squeezing and were now smoothly stroking and, despite the material of her jacket, she could feel the heat, and relived the memory of the afternoon's 'practice' session.

Becca was standing there with her mouth ajar, and Emma summoned a smile—it wasn't huge, but it was a smile. 'First thing possible, Becca? I really will need it first thing.'

'Absolutely.' The receptionist had a reprieve and she appeared to be taking it both hands wide.

Jake's arm slid back across Emma's shoulders and down her arm—where he snagged her hand with his own. Warm and firm, he gave her fingers a gentle squeeze. She felt a matching contraction in her heart and lower belly and she wished she could extricate herself as soon as possible. All this touching was doing crazy things to her insides. None of it was real. She had to remember that.

He turned and spoke, his attention so focussed on her, as if he'd forgotten Becca was even there. 'I'll see you back here in ten, OK? I've just got one more thing to sort out.'

Keenly aware of Becca and her open mouth, Emma had no option but to nod. Jake's eyes were brimming with laughter and she couldn't wait to get him alone to tick him off.

Jake. Alone.

Bad thoughts.

She escaped to the lift and found herself shutting down her computer and packing her briefcase without a second thought of completing the work. She could do it in the morning. She was ahead by anyone else's standards—but she liked to finish well in front of schedule.

Back in the reception area exactly ten minutes later she found him waiting for her, jacket slung over his arm, brilliant smile in place. Becca was handing over to the night receptionist and watching. They left together, Jake holding the door for her as they exited.

He was still beside her five paces down the street and away from the hotel windows.

'What are you doing?'

'Seeing you home.'

'You don't have to. That was just for the benefit of Becca.' Wasn't it?

'No, actually, I really want to see you home.'

Her pulse picked up a little and it wasn't from the walking. 'It's about a ten-minute walk.'

'Really? So is mine. Which way are you?'

Realising she wasn't going to get rid of him, and secretly pleased about it, she set forth in the direction of home.

'Are you in a motel?' she asked. 'You didn't want to stay at Sanctuary?'

He shook his head. 'Needed space from the job. I'm in a serviced apartment. Hagley Towers.'

She knew the building—it was only five minutes' walk from her own place. Several storeys high, it was directly opposite Hagley Park—Christchurch's answer to New York's Central Park. She spent a lot of time walking there and visiting the botanical gardens housed in one section of it, especially at this time of year when the flowers were in bloom. 'Got a nice view?'

'Sure.' He grinned at her. 'Right over the park. And it has a swimming pool, sauna and gym.'

No wonder he looked so trim.

'Where are you?'

'Straight down here and to the left.' She pointed ahead down the busy road.

'You like living so centrally?'

She nodded. She found it handy when she worked such long hours to be within walking distance of the hotel.

'Me too. I have an apartment in the middle of Auckland. A stone's throw from some of the best restaurants in town. Makes deciding what to have for dinner damn hard, doesn't it?' He gave her the grin of a co-conspirator acknowledging a naughty habit.

It was a timely reminder of how different they really were. Of course he'd want to live right in the city so he could make the most of the high life—the bars, clubs and eateries. She bet he had as much trouble deciding which entry in his little black book to invite along to dinner. She just liked being near work. It confirmed her current self-view of boring workaholic. She wished he hadn't wanted to walk with her. He was so attractive, but the more time she spent with him the more she saw how different they were. And how this stupid caper was going to be hard for her. Her discomfort increased with every step as they walked past exclusive boutique shops and cafés.

'We should meet for coffee here some time,' he said chattily. 'You can tell me which of the cafés makes the best brew.'

'How do you like it?'

'Black. Strong.'

Of course. He'd need the hit after those long nights on the town. He'd think she was a complete cream-puff with her decaf soy latte with vanilla shot. Her despondency grew.

Thankfully they arrived at her street. It was an interesting mix of new modern apartments—mostly white and built from combinations of wood, concrete block and plaster. Nestled in and

around were a few remaining examples of the old wooden
cottages that had once dominated the area entirely.

She turned into her gate. He stopped and stared.

'This is your place?'

She nodded. She'd been extremely fortunate. She'd mort-
gaged herself to the hilt as a student to snap it up, but had been
paying it off at an extremely fast rate—the accountant in her
keeping her on the straight and narrow. It needed a lot of work,
but it was hers.

She followed the direction of his gaze, taking in the façade.
'Don't you like it?'

There was a postage-stamp-sized garden in the front. Wisteria
grew up the veranda pole and across decorating half the tiny
cottage with stalactites of lavender petals. Chipped, lichen-
covered terracotta pots crowded the ground and had fragrant
blooms spilling from them. The air was heavy with the scent of
sweet peas and roses.

'Sure I do, it's great. It's just…unexpected. Wow. You're
sitting on a gold-mine, you know.'

She did. Developers would demolish the building and have
two apartments on the tiny square in no time.

Jake was still looking intrigued. 'I thought you'd be in one
like those.'

He pointed over the road to the three units in a row. Sterile,
flat-roofed modern boxes. She thought of them as microwave
houses. She didn't dislike them—part of her admired the clean
lines, and the simple monochromatic landscape architecture
using native grasses, shrubs and river stones. But she loved her
old cottage and its English-country-style pot garden with its
richly scented and deeply coloured flowers.

He was looking at her thoughtfully. His eye ran over her suit
again and she suddenly saw what he was thinking. That her
clean-lined dressing style was far more suited to the clean-lined
architecture across the street. That the slightly crumbling old
wooden cottage with its trailing wisteria was a tad too soft and
sweet to be hers. He saw her in 2D too—up 'til now she'd

thought he didn't, had wanted to think he saw more in her than the stereotypical frigid workaholic Becca had her pegged as. Obviously not. It hurt.

He loitered by the gate. 'Aren't you going to invite me in?'

'Um.' There were things in there she didn't want him to see. Didn't want anyone to see. And she needed to escape his presence for a while. He was used to the casual, relaxed, have-a-laugh type. She was intense. Right now she needed a glass of cool white wine and some time to work on her project and not think or feel—to stamp out this crazy desire that had her body on edge. Her muddled head needed space. So did her heart.

'Actually I've got some things I need to get done. Maybe another time?'

It sounded insincere and cold and she couldn't make it otherwise.

Did she imagine the flash of disappointment in his face?

No. She hardened. He was new to town. It wouldn't be long and he'd be adding names to his black book and he'd lose interest in her and her image. And that would most definitely be for the best. Pretending she didn't care was something Emma was really good at.

CHAPTER FOUR

'LET'S have dinner.'

Jake was determined to get Emma to say yes. He'd been there almost a week and, while he'd seen her several times a day, it wasn't enough.

He went down to the hotel even when he didn't need to—just on the chance he might catch her. Spent the time he was there in a state of anticipation. Told himself it was because he wanted to further develop the 'story' of their relationship, but really he just wanted to further things full stop. He wanted to get to know her. There seemed to be a whole lot more to her than met the eye. Trouble was, she was too good at hiding it.

Each time they passed he looked at her, and took the opportunity to touch her, finding even just the slightest brush incredibly stimulating. Tempting him to want more. But the closer he got, the more he pushed it, the bigger the distance seemed between them. And he found himself caring less and less about whether anyone was watching. He'd already done the job for her. People saw what they wanted to see. He'd read the speculation in the eyes of the other hotel workers. As far as they were concerned, he and Emma were one hot item. Increasingly Jake wished it were true.

She was looking as if she was about to refuse—again. In private she was holding him at arm's length. Then he saw the flash in her eyes, the hint of passion. And he thought for the thousandth time of the kiss they'd shared less than a week ago. She'd let a part of her slip out that night—one he hadn't known was there. Fresh, exciting and wild, and he wanted to find it again. He was pretty certain he could in the four weeks he had left with her, but he knew he needed to take care. She was like a wild flower, beautifully tempting to pick but fragile. Too much force and she'd wither away from him. So he restrained himself—not touching her this time, giving her some space. Hoping she noticed and missed the contact.

'Come on, Emma. Let's just grab a bite and catch up on old times.' The old neighbour approach might be the winner. God, he wanted to win her.

He heard her sigh, and saw her soften. 'We could go to The Strip.'

'The Strip?' He raised his brows suggestively, unable to resist the tease. Old habits died hard.

She coloured. 'It's what they call the area of bars and restaurants down by the river.'

He knew perfectly well what it was and where it was. He just enjoyed seeing how much he could make her blush. It was surprisingly easy. But it wasn't fun; it was arousing. He'd love to do all kinds of things to make her blush.

'OK, let's do The Strip.'

She flashed a look at him and he gave her his best smile of innocence. Neighbourly. Just a hint of naughty.

'Pizza, pasta, rack of lamb?' She gave him the options.

'You choose.'

They walked out of the hotel together as they had done each night that week. Only instead of parting at the street corner to their own places, they walked in the opposite direction to the river. He breathed in the warm wind and glanced at her. She wasn't wearing her jacket, and was just in shirt sleeves. It was nothing like that figure-hugging white number he'd made her reveal the other day, but it wasn't bad. The soft fabric clung to her slim curves. He put the brakes on his thoughts—he needed to play it slow. She felt the attraction but she was cautious. He was counting on her being curious too. And he'd reel her in, nice and gentle.

They sat at a table outside with the warm wind gently teasing wisps of her hair. She always used to wear it up, her pony-tail swinging, a rich brown—the colour of the darkest chocolate. He'd only seen it loose a couple of times and he'd hardly recognised her. More grown-up, more relaxed. He'd love to see her hair out now. Only she tied it all up so he couldn't see even the length of her pony-tail. His fingers itched to test its silkiness. Loosen it. Loosen her.

She toyed with her drink, waiting for their food, waiting for him to say something.

'Remember that day I found you in the park?' He hadn't really intended to sit and reminisce, had been planning more of a charm offensive. But he wanted to talk to her about that day. While he hadn't thought of it in years, in recent days he'd remembered it often. It made him think there was more to Emma than met the eye.

It had been one of the first days of summer. The kind of hot, dry day you dreamed of the entire winter. Sixteen, he'd been down at the park skateboarding with some mates, living it up before the fruit-picking season started. And he'd spotted her sitting camouflaged in the grasses by the creek. Crying. Something about seeing her with her hair scraped back into its usual pony-tail, her face streaked with tears, had pulled at him. He'd been unable to walk on by. The slump in her shoulders had struck him. She'd looked as if she'd carried a burden no kid in their early teens should have to bear. He'd thought something terrible had happened. That someone had hurt her. And in a way someone had.

He'd told the others to go on ahead, not wanting to draw attention to her. He'd slipped back once they were out of sight.

She'd just finished her first year at high school and she'd come home for the holidays, report card in tow. And that was what she'd been upset about. She'd been heartbroken over her report. He'd nearly laughed—report cards had usually been a source of amusement for him. Not life-and-death dramas.

He'd asked to see it and had nearly died when he'd read the results. They'd been awesome and yet she'd said they weren't good enough. She hadn't come first; she hadn't got the best grades across the board. And she hadn't wanted to face her father.

'He said we'd go on a beach holiday if I got top. But I only came top in Art and that doesn't count and so we won't go.'

'Of course you will. He was just trying to encourage you. You've done brilliantly. Far better than I ever have. That Art comment is fantastic.'

Her tears flowed again. 'I'm dropping it next year. Dad thinks it's a waste of time.'

He tried to joke with her, make her see that in the grand scheme it really wasn't that important. That her father would be proud of her no matter what.

But he wasn't and she was right. They hadn't gone on the holiday. Instead she'd been packed off to a maths camp. Her father had stuck to his word. And Jake had wanted to shake some sense into him.

Emma didn't look up, but kept playing with the stem of her glass. For a second he thought she hadn't heard the question, but then he noticed the gentle tide of colour in her cheeks.

'That day I got home from school, you mean? When I was crying?'

'Yeah.'

She looked embarrassed. 'I was so pathetic, wasn't I? Crying over a report card. You must have thought I was such a geek.'

'No. I felt sorry for you.'

He had. He'd even put his arm around her to give her a reassuring hug as he would Sienna. And incredibly he'd felt a pull of attraction. Ripping through his torso, right in his gut. He'd dropped his arm pronto.

In hindsight he knew it to have simply been a touch of lust

aroused by physical closeness. The intensity hadn't been because it was her, but because it had been the first time. Not long after he'd discovered girls who would talk back, smile, flirt and then offer a whole lot more.

He hadn't gone back to school after the summer of the report card. He'd had to get out and work—Sienna had needed his help. If he worked then Mum could have more time caring for her and he could help earn the money for her medical treatment. His father had died prematurely from a heart complaint that Sienna had inherited. He hadn't been going to lose her too. And that had been when he'd had his own run-in with Emma's father. Discovered for himself the height of his expectations. And discovered his own desire to prove the man wrong.

Emma cleared her throat. He looked up to find her eyes on him. A shy honesty peeped out of their greeny-brown depths. 'You were nice to me that day. Usually you threw water bombs over the fence.'

He chuckled. True.

She smiled. 'It was like living next to Dennis the Menace.'

'I wasn't that bad.'

'Not far off.'

He loved the teasing glint in her eye and felt warmed by her relaxation. He leant forward and began a 'do you remember' tale of epic proportions and maximum laughs.

Emma lingered over her dessert, but her mind kept flipping back to that earlier conversation.

I felt sorry for you.

She'd never have expected him to remember that day. She sure as hell hadn't forgotten. That had been the beginning of her crush. Until then he'd been the boy next door who played pranks. Suddenly he'd turned into a real person.

He'd stopped. He'd listened. He'd cared.

No one had done that before. No one had since. No wonder she'd had a thing for him—and still did. One act of kindness that had probably meant nothing to him had affected her for years.

He'd put an arm around her and given her shoulder a squeeze. And she'd wanted to lean in to him. His body hot and damp from the skateboarding. Strong, tanned, already muscular from holiday work spent picking fruit. She'd wanted him to put his other arm around her too. Then she hadn't really known what she'd wanted, she'd just wanted it to last. But it hadn't—he'd let her go abruptly, and she missed the contact immediately. He hadn't stayed much longer. For ages after she'd sat in the grass, not crying any more, not thinking about her grades, but thinking about Jake, and how attractive he'd suddenly become.

She'd rarely seen him after that—she'd been away at school; he'd been working. The odd occasion she had seen him in town he'd always been accompanied by some beautiful, buxom blonde. And she'd never been able to compete.

He'd felt sorry for her. He still did. Great. So that was why he'd suggested their fake fling. Any fantasy of that first kiss having more meaning fled. It wasn't that he was attracted to her. He was just the cool guy helping the ugly duckling do the transformation to pulling princess—but only 'til midnight. The clock was ticking and soon enough she'd be the ugly one again. She was mixing up her fairy tales, but this wasn't a fairy tale. There wouldn't be a happy ending here.

Humiliation killed her appetite. She shouldn't have accepted his dinner invitation. But she couldn't say no any more. She was too tempted and too teased by the touches of the past week. She'd spent those days on tenterhooks, waiting, wondering when he'd appear round the corner next. She'd taken to wandering through the hotel completely unnecessarily—telling herself it was to check on the building work, but that was a complete lie.

And when she did see him it unsettled her so much it was all she could do not to run in the opposite direction. He had that smile just for her, would catch her eye, would stand close and take advantage of the opportunity to touch her—a stroke down her arm, a hand on her shoulder, a brush across the back of her neck. All of it designed to show their intimacy. All of it increasing her desire for more.

She wore short sleeves or sleeveless shirts daily. Her jacket hung gathering dust on the hanger upstairs. And she worked hard to preserve her equilibrium—trying to hide the impact of his actions. It wasn't that she didn't enjoy his attention. She enjoyed it a little too much and she didn't want him to know. That was why she'd kept it short and light, declining any invitations to spend any longer than five minutes with him. More time than that would be too much of a test. But by her agreeing to the scheme to beef up her image, their relationship had already leapt to one of greater intimacy. Them against the others. Sharing secrets, sharing history, sharing a laugh. It made him all the more attractive. That silly teen crush had returned with a vengeance.

And if he knew? He'd felt sorry for her then—he'd feel even more sorry for her now. Socially inept girl fell for guy who was only out to offer a helping hand.

Four weeks to go and, while she didn't want it to end, she couldn't wait 'til it was over.

'Shall we go on and hit the dance floor?'

That was an invitation that had to be refused for more than one reason. She didn't hit the dance floor. Ever. Especially not with the gorgeous guy who already felt sorry for her. If he saw her trying to dance he'd fall in a heap laughing. 'I have a load of work to get through tomorrow.' Work she should have been doing tonight.

'Well, it'll still be there tomorrow, Emma. What about some more fun now?' With that voice and those eyes he could tempt a nun into nudity.

'I'm no good on the dance floor, Jake.'

'Really? I don't believe you. All girls are good on the dance floor.'

All *his* girls would be. But she wasn't. Uncoordinated. It was the geek gene. No avoiding it. She couldn't do the curvy hip-wiggling, boob-jiggling thing. She was too angular. 'You like dancing?'

His eyes were dancing right now. 'Yeah, I like all kinds of dancing.'

He didn't need to say any more. She knew exactly what he was thinking.

The atmosphere thickened, temperature rising. If she let herself, she could believe he was flirting with her. No audience, no ulterior motive. For real and not just neighbourly.

Her whole body seemed to be melting and she suddenly wanted to push it. Test out her intuition. Was he really sending those signals to her? Or was she woolly-headed, merely imagining he was because she wanted it so bad?

She spoke, the breathiness coming naturally. 'What's your favourite?'

He didn't move a muscle, didn't look away, his attention wholly focussed on her. The intensity burned. 'Sometimes I like fast, spontaneous. Other times more leisurely.'

'And if you were dancing with me? What style would you go for then?' Almost bold, but her mouth was dry and inside her heart jack-hammered her ribcage.

'With you?' There was a silence. Neither of them moved, not even an eyelid. 'I'd want to try every which way with you, Emma. But if you're not so sure I might have to start slow, smooth. I'd have to hold you close.'

At the rush of adrenalin she knew she had to step back from the game—she was no match for him. She cleared her throat, hoped the breathiness had gone and that humour replaced it. 'Tango, then.'

He met her banter immediately. 'Shall we find a rose? You can hold it between your teeth.'

She'd been thinking of doing other things with her teeth, lips and tongue. 'I'm not a rose person.'

'No? What are you, then?

'A daisy.'

'No way.'

'I am. A particular daisy, though.'

He raised his brows. 'You have me intrigued.'

'Yep, and you're a tulip. Red tulip.'

He laughed outright then. But she knew things he didn't. She smiled at his relaxing demeanour. The scorching moment had passed and now she couldn't be sure if it had happened at all—if the message in his eyes had been the one she'd wanted to read.

A gang of slightly worse-for-wear party-goers wandered past along the road. They tried and failed to gain entry to the bar. It reminded her how late it was getting.

'I really should get going. I do have a lot to do tomorrow.'

'All right, Miss Conscientious. I'll walk you home.'

'You don't need to. It's still light, I'll be perfectly safe.'

'No, I'll see you there.'

'It's out of your way. Your place is nearer.'

'Unless you're planning on staying the night at my place, I'm walking you home.'

The desire to be brazen resurged, but she hoped the dusk would hide her heated cheeks and played safe. 'It's a nice night for a walk.'

His teeth flashed white in his wide smile.

She tried to suppress the tickle of pleasure and failed.

The wind had dropped, but the temperature was still warm as they gently strolled alongside the river. He walked near enough to her that their arms brushed ever so slightly every now and then, sending sparks through her. She wished they were lovers, so she could touch him as much as she wanted at any time and not have to rely on these accidental moments. She wondered if he was as aware of her nearness as she was his. Daydreaming.

Her nerves tightened with every step towards home. Would he ask her to invite him in again? He had been flirting with her; he had. But this wasn't a date. This was a dinner with an old friend. Not even that, an old neighbour. OK, her pretend lover. Confused about what they were doing—what was real and what wasn't—she opened her gate and found him hot on her heels right up the garden path.

She paused by the door feeling uncomfortable, and made a show of fossicking in her bag for her keys so that she could delay looking up at him. Her breathing was shorter. They'd kissed once and she wanted to again. She could hardly believe how easily that had happened that first night. Now it seemed impossible.

She turned and put the key in the door, battling with the rattling lock.

He stood right behind her, so close she could feel the heat from him; there must only be an inch between them. She leaned a little closer to the door to stop herself leaning back against him.

'What's the problem?'

'I'm having trouble with the door handle. It keeps coming off.'

'I'll fix it for you.'

'It's OK.'

'It's a security issue. I'll fix it first thing.'

First thing? Would he still be here then? She fumbled some more. He stepped around her, to rest against the wall of the cottage, still temptingly near.

She looked at him, the 'you don't have to' dying on her tongue as she saw he was waiting for her to say exactly that. So she didn't. Instead she smiled. 'Thank you.'

His expression revealed his surprise, and his amusement. 'It was fun tonight, Emma. It was nice spending time with you.'

She looked away, her smile dying. *Nice*. Almost as bad as 'I felt sorry for you.' This *was* dinner with an old neighbour.

'Right. Same. Thanks for dinner.' She wished she had the chutzpah she'd had only a week ago. To flirt in the way that had prompted him to instigate that kiss. But the more time she spent around him, the more she wanted him, and the less able she felt to put herself out to get him. For him it was all fake. But she couldn't help her reaction to his proximity. Her gaze dropped to his mouth.

'Goodnight.' He spoke briskly. She looked to his eyes and saw his intent, serious expression. It was almost a frown and she was about to ask what was wrong when his lips twisted into a smile that was a shadow of its usual brilliance. 'See you soon.'

He quickly stepped away, hands jammed in pockets. She stood on the deck listening as his unwavering footsteps grew fainter, wondering why a goodnight kiss hadn't even been anywhere near the agenda, and telling herself she wasn't disappointed.

She rose early as usual, despite the fact she'd taken for ever to get to sleep. Unable to get the image of Jake from her mind—his teasing comments and devilish nature—she'd lain and looked at her ceiling for hours. She might not have that much experience, but she wasn't a complete idiot and Jake had been making a play for her. Right up to her front door when everything had stopped. As if the brakes had been thrown on.

She tried not to make too much of it. Of course he'd flirted. That was what Jake did. He couldn't help himself. It didn't mean anything. He was just carrying their act on a little—giving her some more practice. Being charming. Flattering. And it definitely was fake because if he'd meant it, he'd have kissed her right there on the doorstep. Instead he was careful not to. She guessed he didn't want to lead her on. More humiliation.

She pulled on some clothes and went to her studio to do some work, to make the most of the soft morning light and to banish the moroseness that came with the knowledge that Jake wasn't interested.

Two hours later it was barely past eight and someone was banging the knocker on her door repeatedly. She jerked her head up, having been concentrating so hard on the page before her she hadn't seen anyone come up the path. Whoever it was wasn't going away.

'OK!' she called out, hoping it wasn't some life-or-death emergency, but the way the knocker was being abused she began to wonder. She slid back the chain and opened the door.

Jake, in those faded blue jeans of the first night, hair still damp, unshaven and edgy. Energy almost bursting from his skin.

'I said I'd—' He broke off, his gaze trailing over her—top to toe and back. Then again—this time stopping just above her middle. Then he looked up to her face. 'You look really different.' His voice sounded froggy.

Incredibly aware of the fact she hadn't bothered putting any underwear on, she went for diversion. 'It's my hair.' She hadn't done it. Just pulled on top and shorts and settled straight to work. So it hung loose, shaggy, the fresh-out-of-bed look. She went to pull it back and tie it with the elastic band on her wrist.

'No, don't. Leave it.' He spoke briskly and she stopped, her arms mid-air. His eyes burned into her. 'It looks nice.'

Nice. Again. But the meaning seemed different this time.

She lowered her arms. The silence was small but sultry and she felt the change. As if the wind had shifted from a chilly easterly to warm nor'west. The wind of madness.

There was nothing neighbourly about her feelings right now. He looked too intense, too tempting, and her response was too terrifying. She looked at the large box his hand gripped tightly. He followed the direction of her gaze.

'A man never goes anywhere without his toolbox.'

'Is that right?' Her soft whisper was more of a challenge than she'd intended.

He answered with a slow, seductive smile. 'It's always good to be prepared.'

'I'll bear that in mind.' Still soft, sort of sassy and slightly cynical. She congratulated herself on keeping cool.

His smile widened and the tease flashed in his eyes. 'I said I'd fix the door first thing. You can fix me some food after to say thank you.'

There were other, more exciting ways of saying thank you. Every one of them flashed through her mind. Her cool persona evaporated. She blinked. 'OK.'

He put the toolbox down and bent at the knees to open it, showcasing muscular thighs. She stood for a moment taking in the god literally at her feet, then slipped inside and made a calming pot of tea. Holding the mug in her hands, she couldn't resist loitering in the hallway to watch as he started work on the door. Framed in the light, he looked like every woman's handyman fantasy. His shirt was open and he had a white singlet on underneath. She wished it were three hours later and five degrees warmer so he'd take the shirt off. He glanced over and saw her watching, saw her drinking.

He walked down the little hallway towards her. 'Can I have some?'

Some what? Some of her?

He took the mug from her fingers and had a sip, not taking his eyes from her. Then he frowned. 'Hell, what is this muck?'

She laughed. 'Herbal tea. Good for your brain.'

'Got any coffee? *Real* coffee?'

'What's that good for?'

'Energy. Lots of energy.'

He was joking with her again. She liked it—the tease of one shimmy forward, one step back. A little flirty dance and, sucker for punishment that she was, she shimmied. 'You need more energy?'

'I'm thinking it might come in handy.'

The provocation in his eyes warmed her already steamy thoughts. She'd have the energy for anything he was up for—with or without the coffee. A kiss would be a good start. She stared at him, at the generous curve of his mouth. Did she just lean forward towards him? Offer him her mouth? Take his hand and lead him straight to her small bedroom at the back of the house? What would Becca do? Simply say, 'Hey, how about it?'

She wished she had the confidence to do all that and more. Wished she could just tell him. Instead she stepped back. 'I'm just going to nip to the shop round the corner for some things for breakfast. Back in ten, OK?'

Jake nodded and forced his attention back to the door handle. He'd managed to spin a fifteen-minute job into forty. She looked stunning. Stunningly different from her weekday wear—the buttoned-up suit. Today she wore a pair of ancient-looking shorts that revealed her slim legs. And a skimpy singlet top—hot pink with splashes of who knew what on it. Skin, skin, skin. Acres of it and he wanted to touch so bad. He tried really, really hard not to dwell on the fact that she wasn't wearing a bra, but it was like a neon sign flashing in his head.

And her hair. It hung to her shoulders framing her face looking more beautiful than he'd imagined, and he ached to touch it. Could imagine it brushing his face as she leaned over him. How he wanted her.

It hadn't been that long since he'd been with a woman—it was never long for Jake—but he had a hunger in him that was growing every day. And aside from the crippling physical attraction, he liked her company, plain and simple. She was bright, humorous and fun to be around, and there was nowhere else he wanted to be right now than in her little cottage doorway, just hanging out.

Except in her bed.

He watched as she walked out the gate and turned down the footpath, out of sight, infinitely more relaxed. She was talking back to him, a cute little sass that he loved. Had it been his imagination or had she almost leaned forward for a kiss in the hallway just then? Talk about wishful thinking. But with her lips parted, her face illuminated, there had been invitation in her eyes.

Then it had gone.

So, so close, and he'd be damned if he was leaving her house today without some sort of contact.

CHAPTER FIVE

THE walk to the shop and back provided Emma with some essential oxygen to the brain. Enabled her to think. She strode out, trying to grow her confidence with every step. She wanted to be like any other red-blooded woman and have an affair with the really hot guy she'd had a thing for since her teens.

She gave herself the pep talk. Don't over analyse. Don't worry about what may or may not happen. Why not just have fun? Flirt. Just do it.

She tried to swallow the performance anxiety.

He had a wealth of experience. She had nil.

He was used to curvy blondes. She was an ironing-board brunette.

But the spark was there. And she was going to blow on it. Be normal. Go for something she really wanted. Jake. Just once. Just for herself.

Although she'd yet to figure out quite how.

He was sitting on the bottom step of the verandah when she returned. She carried the tray of two large, strong black coffees and two decaf, soy lattes with vanilla shot, and had the carrier bag of groceries looped over her arm. She paused on the step and offered him one of the coffees.

He took it with glee. 'You're an angel.'

'I didn't think you'd want any of my instant decaf.'

He looked appalled. 'Hell, no.'

He followed her inside and into the kitchen where she set about preparing their meal.

'So no *real* coffee, you don't smoke and I'm betting you don't drink that much—apart from wine, which we both know doesn't count.'

She smiled. They'd grown up in the heart of the wine country of New Zealand where the wine practically flowed out of the kitchen tap. Even so, cheap drunk was the phrase to describe her.

'Don't you have any vices? No secret indulgence?'

'Chocolate. Clichéd but true.'

'I'm guessing the real seventy-per-cent bitter stuff.'

She giggled. 'No. Caramello actually. A bar a day. Vitamin C.'

He came and leaned against the bench where she was working. She concentrated extra hard to keep her hand steady as she wielded her large kitchen knife. He stood so close she could smell his musky scent.

'Can I help at all?'

It would help if he'd keep just a wee bit more of a distance. Either that or no distance at all. This so-close-but-not-actually-connecting thing was doing her head in.

'No, it won't take a minute. You just sit and watch.'

He didn't take the hint. Didn't sit. Stayed right where he was—right beside her. If she waggled her elbow just a tad she'd touch him. Not nearly good enough.

Intensely aware of his scrutiny, she deftly cut the Portobello mushrooms into thick slices, halved the tomatoes and separated the small breakfast sausages. She turned away from him, breathing out in relief, and put the large frying-pan on the hob. She splashed in some oil and a decent knob of butter, allowing it to melt before putting in streaky bacon from the fridge and the just-chopped food.

He breathed in deeply. 'That smells so good. I never imagined you'd eat like this. You're like a short-order cook.'

She smiled, poking at the mushrooms with a wooden spoon. 'I love a cooked breakfast. It's my speciality.'

'Really?'

'Yeah, it's what I serve up if I'm having people over to dinner. It's the only thing I can really cook.'

'I don't believe that.'

'OK, it's the only thing I really like to cook. Fast. Satisfying.'

While the food in the fry-pan sizzled she whisked a few eggs with a fork, adding a grate of cheese and a dash of milk to the bowl. 'I cheat, though. I scramble the egg in the microwave and the hash browns are from the freezer.'

'Looks pretty good to me.'

She put some bread in the toaster and pushed the lever down. Two minutes later she was spreading the hot toast with butter and piling scrambled egg on top.

'I thought you'd be a cereal and skimmed milk person.'

She snorted. 'Cardboard. Breakfast is my most important meal.'

'You have this every day?'

'Not with all the trimmings. But a good breakfast, yeah. Sometimes I don't get time for lunch.'

'You work through so it's just a bar of Caramello.' His glance stabbed.

She laughed. 'Don't look so disapproving. It's not like you don't work hard.'

'Yeah, but at least I have some balance in my life.' Vitality, virility, she knew his kind of balance.

'I have balance.' She might not be out dating a different man every other night, but she did have her own passion in life. She just kept it to herself, that was all.

In the ten minutes since she'd walked back in the door breakfast had been prepared, cooked and was now plated up on the bench in the kitchen, waiting to be demolished. She grabbed cutlery from the drawer and picked up one of the plates.

'Let's eat on the verandah.'

She led the way as he snagged the other plate and the tray with the remaining coffees. Out on the corner of the verandah in the shade stood her table and two chairs. An old but super-comfortable sofa sat under the window. Pots full of flowering plants decorated the border. Their perfume rich but not overpowering. She took one of the chairs and watched as Jake sat and started consuming with enthusiasm.

'Now I know about this I'm thinking about breakfasting with you every day, Emma.'

She paused, fork halfway to her mouth, as she imagined the scenario. Breakfast. In bed? With what on the menu—her?

She had to stop these thoughts. Everything he said she managed to read a hidden meaning into.

He slowed as he reduced the pile of food, sighing happily. 'It's a great place you have here. You like living alone?'

She looked out at the pretty garden, the stunning backdrop of architecturally designed town houses. 'Yes. I work long hours. It's nice to come home and be able to relax, do my own thing.'

'What do you do to relax?'

She looked sideways at him, but he seemed genuinely interested. It wasn't a tease. 'This and that. Potter in my garden.'

'Yeah, it's beautiful.' He reached out to the pot nearest his leg, touching the petals of the hyacinth it housed.

She watched the softness of his stroke. 'It's small, easy to manage.' Truth be told, all she had to do was water it. The beauty of a pot garden was it didn't need weeding—a good thing as she didn't have time; she was too busy on her this and that.

She sat back, replete and warm in the morning sun, determinedly looking away from him. Ordinarily she'd make like a cat, curl up on the sofa and doze for ten. But today an extreme quantity of adrenalin ran through her veins. She might want to go to bed, but sleeping wasn't on the activity list once there.

Out of the corner of her eye she saw him lift his arms, pointing his elbows at the sky while his hands fisted at his neck. He stretched, curving his spine to one side, then the other. He groaned. 'You gotta help me burn off some of this energy. Two coffees and all that food.'

So the meal hadn't made him sluggish either. Did he want to burn it up in the way she wanted to? 'What did you have in mind?'

He stared into the middle distance, seemingly transfixed by a purple iris. 'How about a walk round the park?'

Curbing her disappointment, she fixed a bright smile on her face. 'Sure.'

He picked up the plates and transported them back to the kitchen while she kicked off her flip-flops and laced her trainers. She stepped into the bathroom and was about to tie up her hair before she thought better of it. She dragged a comb through the worst of the tangles and then simply used her fingers to smooth it. She turned away from the mirror—not wanting to see the heightened colour in her cheeks, the anticipation in her eyes.

After checking the curtains were shut in her workroom and the door was closed tight she went into the kitchen to find him just finishing the dishes and wiping down the bench.

'Thanks for that—you didn't have to.'

'Least I could do after that meal. It doesn't take a minute. I always did the dishes for Mum.'

He would have too. Loyal. Protective. He might not take his relationships with women seriously, but Emma knew there were two women in his life he'd do anything for. Had done everything for—his mother and his sister. After both his father and grand-father died Jake was the man in the family—age sixteen. It hadn't been long after that he left school. For all his joking around there was another side to him. The man who took those responsibilities seriously, especially Sienna, the sister he'd nearly lost. He was looking at her questioningly and she realised she'd been staring. 'Let's go,' she said, quickly leading the way out.

Saturday morning and Hagley Park was busy with runners, rollerbladers and parents pushing prams. The last of the bluebells could be seen in the meadow across the road. They walked on one of the many paths crossing the park, strolling easily, neither of them really wanting to pace it out.

'So you think your women at the hotel are seeing you in a different light?' No smile as he asked.

She was sure of it. So was everyone else. Dan the doorman had winked at her the other day and usually he'd barely meet her eyes.

'Yes. I think they think I'm actually human now.'

'Oh, you're very human.' He spoke softly.

She tried to quell her overly sensitive awareness. 'In that I make mistakes, absolutely.'

'You think it was a mistake? I thought it was kinda fun.'

Her heart dropped. *Was. Fun.* Just a game and over already.

But then he spoke again, low and slow. 'All that touching, flirting, being close.'

'Yes.' She whispered it so softly she was sure he wouldn't hear.

He stopped walking. So attuned to him, she stopped in almost the same instant. She stared up at him and his expression was as serious as she knew hers to be. He reached out and ran his fingers down the length of her arm to take her hand. He pulled her with him as he walked off the path, into the trees. He said nothing. She said nothing. He led her into the shade of a tree, ducking under the large, low branches into the secret space by its strong trunk. He turned and leaned against it, facing her and still holding her hand tightly, keeping her in front of him.

They were protected by the branches and the sound of the traffic was muted, the other park users hidden from sight. It felt as if there were only the two of them in the world. And the spark was enough to send a whole forest in flames.

He looked at her mouth, and then back to her eyes. A rueful expression mingled with the blazing gaze. 'I can't stand it any more, Emma. I'm going to have to kiss you.'

Somehow, even though she was sure she wasn't breathing, she answered, 'What about your rules?'

The pressure on her hand tightened, and he pulled her a little closer.

'There's no audience. No ulterior motives. Just…desire.'

The very same desire rippled through her. And the thrill she got from his admission fuelled her saucy question. 'What about the clothes?'

The corners of his mouth twitched in that delightful fashion that had her wanting to taste them, feel the humour. 'Well, two out of three isn't bad.'

She tried to think of a pert reply. 'But I'm a perfectionist, Jake. I like to get one hundred per cent.' Quite where she got the audacity to say that, she didn't know. Maybe it was heatstroke caused by the burn in his eyes.

He pulled her closer still, his hand relinquishing hers, but only to slide around her waist. 'You'll get one hundred per cent, Emma. Trust me.'

She was incapable of further speech. Her mouth parted as she stared up at him. Riveted by the heat in his eyes, the humour in his expression, she waited, wanting to lean that further fraction forward to bring them into length-to-length contact. But she felt hesitation in him.

He spoke. 'I've been wanting a repeat of that kiss the other night all week. There's no one watching now, Emma. Do you really want it this time?'

Everything inside seemed to have liquefied. A sweet melting sensation that made her want to spread her pliant body over his hard one. There was only one thing to say. 'Yes.'

Her lids lowered as his head bent even as she answered. She felt the increase of pressure from his arms as they tightened around her, as if he were afraid she'd step away. As if. Instead she stepped closer, tilted her head so she was right there for him.

Contact.

There was no gentle testing of the waters this time. Mouths open, tongues searching, deeply taking. She loved the roughness of his stubble as he moved against her. She raised her hands, threaded them through his thick hair and held him as she kissed him back. Hard. Heavenly and highly addictive.

His hands lifted from her waist, sweeping from her shoulder blades down her body. She felt their fire through her thin singlet top. And even that thin covering was too much. Skin. She wanted it bare.

The warmth in her belly sharpened to a desperate ache. She

wanted this so much. But she wanted so much more than this. One hundred per cent.

She pressed against him. His tightness soothed her a little. She pressed again, tilting her hips forward so they ground against him. A wash of heat dizzied her as she felt his erection, large and hard. Her mouth parted further as the moan escaped. She curled her fingers tighter in his hair, fixing him there as she pressed again. Again. And again.

He jerked his head back. 'Stop.'

'What?' Confused, she looked up at him. The flames racing in her veins turned to ice in an instant. Panic. Had she done something wrong?

'If we don't stop now, we won't be stopping at all and we'll get done for indecency.' His fingers dug into her as he grasped her hips and held her away from him. 'Just a kiss with you is lethal. Whatever you do, you really do the best, don't you?'

The way he said it she wasn't sure if this was a good thing or not.

He ran his fingers through his hair—leaving it even more tousled than from when she'd dealt with it. Then he grimaced. 'Let's go back to your house.'

And pick up where they just left off? Yes, please.

'I need to pick up my toolbox before I go home.' He spoke flatly, not looking at her as he dragged a long breath in through his nostrils.

They slowly walked back. She didn't know how to break the silence. Didn't want to do the girl thing and ask to talk about what had just happened. Find out what, if anything, it meant. Find out why she was getting the frosty treatment now. Utterly confused, but she refused to over-analyse, daydream, wish.

He stared straight ahead. His easy humour apparently having gone on holiday. All she knew was she didn't want him to just pick up his box and go. She didn't know what had gone wrong, but she needed to buy some time to make it right. 'Would you be able to do me a favour?'

'Sure.' The automatic response.

'The latch on one of the windows round the back is loose too. Would you mind looking at it?'

The muscle in his jaw twitched. 'Emma, you know what you've just done? You're actually *asking* for help? This has got to be some kind of record.'

She blinked, unprepared for his sarcasm. 'Why do you say that?

'Oh, come on, Emma, you're Miss Independent. You work, work, work and seem like you don't need anything or anybody.'

'I have to work hard,' she replied softly, in contrast to his bark. 'It's expected.'

It was what she'd had to do to get her father's attention. She'd literally had to win his approval. Get an A in Economics and I'll take you to dinner, Emma. Get three A's and I'll buy you a car. Any reward—emotional, material—came from achievement.

He sighed, stretching his fingers from where they were fisted at his sides. 'Yeah, if you don't mind my saying, your dad's real pushy.'

'He wants what's best for me.'

'What you think is best for you, or what he thinks is best for you?'

At that she stopped walking and turned to look at him. 'Who are you to judge, Jake?'

His hands lifted. 'I'm not judging. That's just how it seems. You push yourself to crazy limits to please your father all your life and now you do the same for Max.'

Her jaw fell open. 'Max has been wonderful to me. I owe him a lot.' Why wouldn't she work hard for him?

'Max is your boss and I hope he pays you the earth for the job he asks of you.'

'You think he's taking advantage of me?' She felt stunned.

'Of your type, yeah, maybe. You have to please, Emma. You want people to like you, fair enough, we all do, but you put what others ask ahead of your own wants because it's more important to you to have their approval than it is to satisfy your own dreams.'

'That's rubbish. This is my dream. I've worked damn hard to get where I am. Would I really work so hard if I didn't want it?' Her defence button was well and truly pushed. Where was this coming from?

'Sure, you think you want it. But do you really? Isn't there something else you'd rather be doing?'

She felt the blood rush from her head to her heart. 'What are you on about, Jake? What do you know?'

She saw him do a double take. She realised he'd been shooting in the dark and just happened to hit target. She took a few deep breaths to recover herself. He knew nothing. Of course he didn't. That was impossible. The only person she'd ever shared her silly dreams with was Lucy, and she knew enough of her sister's own secrets to be sure she'd never rat on her. This was just Jake stirring for the sake of it, because for whatever reason he had a serious case of the grumps right now. He must really be regretting kissing her. Anger kicked in her gut. Who was he to kiss her like that and then start digging at her? If he didn't want her, fine; he didn't have to turn into a grizzly bear because things had happened that he didn't like. Hell, he was the one who'd started it.

But she wasn't going to let him know how he'd thrown her. Instead she'd take on his job and lighten things up. Turn the last five minutes into a joke. She racked her brains and then remembered a slogan she'd once read on a tee shirt. 'If you like the look of my peaches, don't shake my tree.' She threw him a tart look, turned and managed a passable saunter away.

Jake watched her sweet rear sashay away from him and couldn't contain the chuckle. The irrational anger he'd felt at his reaction to her was draining. Playful and provocative, she was testing her wings with him and if he was honest with himself he'd say he was happy to be on the flight. More than happy. It was an element of her he'd never suspected. But then, what did he really know of her? Only the achievements her parents had proclaimed to the world, only the hint in her eyes of depths that had yet to be plumbed, only that she was beautiful and when he held her against him she melted and his reason nearly drowned. *That* was where the problem came in. Since when did he seriously contemplate having sex in the middle of a public park in the middle of the day? Since when did he shake with need as he had just then? Since when did he want a woman more than he wanted to breathe? He was familiar with lust—but not like this. Never like this.

And there was more to her. He'd hit on something just then and she'd skirted around it big style. He really wanted to know, had read the panic on her face. Emma the parent-pleaser, the teacher-pleaser…the lover-pleaser? How he'd love to find out. Even more he wanted to find out what would please *her*.

He strolled after her, catching up to her in a few steps. He reached out, couldn't help but slide his arms around her to turn her to face him, only just managing not to haul her close.

He fell back on his humour. 'I wasn't thinking of shaking your tree, honey.'

'No?' She was going for flirty confidence but he could see the uncertain, shy girl in her eye. He loved the mix.

'No, I was planning on making the whole earth move.'

'Really.'

Her soft laugh only made him want her more. Made him want to make it really happen despite the fact that she threatened his self-control completely.

'How were you going to do that?'

'Shall I show you?' Slowly he slid his hands down past the band of her shorts to cup her bottom. Skin on skin. Her eyes widened. He shouldn't. But there was no audience, no ulterior motive, and he couldn't stop. His fingers burned.

He'd really thought he could just mess around. Have some fun while in town. Could sense that with some encouragement, she'd be keen. He'd deliberately stepped back from kissing her last night—figuring a little time would bring her out more. He had wanted to test his own outrageous response to her—wanted to know he could pull back.

He'd paid the price with a sleepless night and a hard body. He'd turned up first thing because he couldn't keep away any longer. And when he had kissed her just then, she'd turned the tables on him. Reality had slipped. His identity had slipped. He'd forgotten who he was and where he was. Forgotten everything but her, the feel of her, what she was doing and how he felt as she did it.

As with everything she did she set the standard. This game belonged in the Olympic arena whereas he was more accustomed to the social-tournament level. Trust Emma to play with an unsurpassable intensity.

He didn't like it. He'd lashed out at her just now—uncharacteristically unsettled. But he couldn't walk away. Temptation and desire had him caught and all he could do was try to stay in charge—of himself.

He hadn't been joking when he'd said he wouldn't be able to stop. It was only supposed to have been a kiss but his body had raced ahead to the ultimate conclusion. Mentally he'd had her stripped and underneath him.

The silky feel of her gentle curves under his hands caused an acceleration of his heart, making him feel as if he'd just ended a two-hour workout. And he was only holding her. OK, so his hands were on her bare skin, but he was fighting the urge to move them, to slide around and stroke her intimately. He ached to feel her wet.

He stared at her luminous eyes—the dark centre reflecting desire. The electric surge in his body warned him again.

'Later, Emma.' He coughed away the rasp. 'I'm going to have to show you later.'

He nearly threw all caution to the wind. Willing to run the risk of getting caught and prosecuted when he saw her disappointment. He couldn't help but give a gentle squeeze. 'We're playing by *all* the rules next time.'

He felt her responsive wriggle and hastily pulled his hands out, stepping away from her. Walking out of the trees towards the road. And damn well determined there would be a next time. Soon.

It shouldn't be feeling this good.

* * *

The latch on the window was old and rusty and wouldn't take a minute to remove. He frowned. 'This is really unsafe, Emma. It's child's play for someone to break in.' The thought of her vulnerability put his anger back on the boil.

He worked on the lock. 'I'm checking all the others before I leave, OK?'

He hardly heard her reply. Glowering, he took his frustration out on the rusty screws. He was shaken by the desire for her, annoyed at the way it had made him lash out at her. She'd been forced to over-achieve, over-please. He'd never much liked Emma's father—hadn't liked the way he'd go on about his daughters. He treated them like performing monkeys—showing off Emma's academic prowess, Lucy's violin-playing. Jake's low opinion had been confirmed after that day he'd found Emma in the park, terrified about the report card any normal person would think was brilliant. His utter dislike had been cemented after he'd had his own brush with him not long after. He'd decided to quit school. Lucas Delaney had come and seen him in the workshop above the garage where his grandfather had taught him to work wood.

He'd lectured. 'You leave school now, you'll be nothing. Picking fruit the rest of your life. Working as a building labourer. Going nowhere fast.'

Jake felt a boy's anger and a man's responsibility. He was nearly seventeen. His mum had been working three jobs, scrimping, saving so she could be there for him and his sister. So Sienna could get the best possible care. Now he was old enough to help out. She needed him. Sienna needed him. And this man had no idea, no understanding of their situation. Having Delaney the Dictator come and blast him was the last thing he needed.

They looked out the window and saw Emma walking across the lawn. 'You see Emma. She knows what she has to do. She's an achiever. She won't be here wasting her talents. You want to go places, you have to put in the work. Quitters don't get anywhere.'

The episode over her report card was still fresh in Jake's

mind. It compounded his determination to prove the man wrong, stoking the fire in his belly to get out there and get on with it.

He had a plan and wasting more time at school for nothing wasn't part of it. He knew what he wanted to do, where he wanted to go.

And he'd done it. In a way Lucas had been right—you had to put in the work. Jake had worked like a dog—physically, mentally. Now he had it—the money, the security and the pleasure of knowing his mother didn't have to work ever again unless she wanted to. Of course, being her, she wanted to. He'd paid off her house, paid for overseas holidays. Most importantly he'd ensured Sienna had had the best possible treatment and now had the best possible outlook. He'd even paid her university fees—not that she seemed that thrilled with his interference these days.

He'd never spoken with Lucas Delaney again.

Jake put the new screws in and tightened them hard, then moved on to inspect the next window. Emma had worked like a dog too. All to gain approval. And she'd paid a price. Her lack of social life and her uptight exterior showed that. Surely she wanted more. She worked too hard to have fun and it irritated him beyond belief. He paused, screwdriver in hand, but that was where he could help out—make her have some fun, for real. That kiss in the park had been very, very real. He'd tapped into her sassy vein already. He chuckled again over her peaches, and wanted to shake her tree so bad. Just so long as *he* could handle it.

He walked round to the front of the cottage. The curtains were drawn on the windows on the left-hand side of the hallway. He stared for a moment. Her bedroom was the small room next to the kitchen at the back and the kitchen had a sitting area that she obviously used as her living room. So what was this room for? The builder in him knew it would be larger than the one at the back and it certainly would be the sunniest room in the house. Wouldn't she want that one for her bedroom?

Curiosity lifted its head and sniffed.

He walked in through the front door. Cocking his head, he

listened in the little hallway. No sight or sound of Emma. He took another step into the house and saw the door to the bathroom was closed. Luck was on his side.

The scent of fresh flowers was even stronger as he opened the door to the front room. He looked about, his eye taking it all in. Wow. So there was something to know.

CHAPTER SIX

THE room was painted white. The floor was bare—the carpet had been ripped up to reveal the wooden boards underneath, but they hadn't been polished. They were still rough with patches of carpet glue evident. Little furniture. A table against the far wall. A chair.

And in the middle of the room, positioned to catch the light from the window, stood a large easel.

Art.

He closed his eyes a second. Remembering. Her best subject on her report card that day in the park. The subject she'd come top in. The subject she'd said she'd have to drop.

Despite the drawn curtains enough light filtered into the room for him to see the paintings that hung over all the walls. On the table spread out were technical-looking drawings—showing the cross-section of a flower. Then he noticed the paraphernalia next to them. The glass slides, the sharp knives, the magnifying glass. On one corner of the table stood pens, pencils. Under the table stood jars full of brushes, canvas being stretched, more paintings—some finished, some looking as if they'd been abandoned halfway. The faint smell of turps mingled with the blossoms that stood in a vase on the small table the far side of the easel.

He moved to stand in the centre of the room and slowly took in the paintings, also studying the drawings neatly laid out on the table. The contrast between the large, flowing paintings on the wall and the tiny, perfect technical drawings was fascinating. Like two halves of the one, the analytical perfectionist creating photographic-like miniatures, and the emotional, sensual person producing paintings that seemed to catch the soul of the flower. His heart, his body swelled.

He heard the step behind him, the closing of the door. He should feel guilty, he really should, but all he felt was awe.

He turned to face her. She'd changed, out of the pink singlet top that he now knew to have been splashed with paint. She'd replaced it with a clinging spring dress with thin straps. She still wasn't wearing a bra. The attraction to her magnified—overwhelming.

'What are you doing in here?'

He didn't even think to use the window latches as an excuse. 'Couldn't help it. It's the sunniest room in the house. I couldn't understand why you weren't using it.'

She was very pale.

His gaze dropped to her hands. Small, fine, perfectly proportioned. Just like her drawings.

'I thought you gave up Art at school.'

'I did.' She took a breath and then words tumbled out. 'I did Economics instead. But I was boarding and the art teacher was nice to me. And she lent me books and let me work in the art classroom after school hours. Basically she tutored me privately. It was our secret.'

'Your dad never knew.'

She shook her head. 'No one knows.'

'Still?'

She looked defiant. 'It's mine.' She glanced around the walls anxiety etched on her face. 'Lucy knows a bit.'

He nodded. He'd guessed the sisters were close. They'd have to or else the competition their father encouraged between them would have destroyed any kind of sibling relationship.

'They're amazing, Emma.'

'I never did get past "Still Life with Flowers",' she said sheepishly as she paced about. 'Come on, let's go.' She looked at him and he knew she wanted him out of there.

No chance.

He looked back to study the drawings on the table, determined not to meet her eyes so he wouldn't see the entreaty there. There was a pile of drawings and next to it a loose sheaf of papers with text on them. He picked it up. There was a list of flowers and blurb written underneath. She had scrawled notes next to each entry. He examined it closer, reading, half forgetting Emma's anxiety as he became engrossed.

Emma stood in the middle of the room, heart thundering. Wanting him out of there but not knowing how she was going to do it. He had the look of a man who wasn't going anywhere without a fight and it wasn't as if she could pick him up and eject him physically. Besides, part of her was fascinated, keen to know his view. She swallowed the rising nerves. Eager for his approval.

She blinked back the sudden tears. He'd been right earlier. She did like to please people. Did want people to think the best of her. Needed to be the best—had to be. And that was why she'd never shared this with anyone. She didn't want that pressure. Didn't want to put this out for judgment. It was her escape, her enjoyment. If she wanted to paint the sky purple behind bright orange daisies, she could. And if she wanted to draw a lily with as much exactness as she could then she'd do that too.

'What is it?' He held Margaret's manuscript, flipping through it and reading her notes and then looking at the drawings Emma had laid out in order on the table.

She stared at his back, the broad shoulders that tapered to slim hips. He was strong and suddenly she wanted a part of that strength. So she snatched a breath and told him something she hadn't told anyone, not even her sister. 'My lecturer has written a book about floriography and asked me to provide some sample illustrations for it.'

'Flori-what?' He finally turned to look at her.

'Floriography.' She stepped up to the table next to him. 'The language of flowers. A Victorian thing. They assigned meanings to flowers so they could pass messages to each other by the flowers they gave to each other.'

'Since when does a commerce lecturer write a book about flowers?'

'Not commerce. Botany.'

'Botany? You studied botany as part of your commerce degree?'

'No, I also did a science degree majoring in plant biology.'

'What?'

'I did a double degree.'

'I didn't know that. Surely I should know that. Your father would have told everyone.'

'He doesn't know.'

'What?'

'He doesn't know.'

'You did a whole other degree and he doesn't know?'

It was why she had such a nil social life. She'd spent every waking moment at university running from lectures to laboratories. Her classmates had spent hours in the cafés and bars while she'd worked on through the night to keep up her drawing as well. She would have done Fine Arts if she could. But the demands of the two degrees had been too great. And she hadn't kept up her formal art education at school. Hadn't had the portfolio required. So she'd compromised and done Botany.

She hovered as he leant over the table, studying the drawings, reading the common and botanical names she'd written in a swirl underneath—and the romantic meaning historically assigned. She'd spent hours over them.

She gabbled, wanting him to understand. 'She's selected mostly common garden flowers and included bits on how to grow them and a bit on creating pretty, meaningful displays with them. It's quite detailed. She wants it to be a little coffee-table book, or a gift book, you know?'

He stood up and faced her, eyes shining. 'Emma, this is brilliant. Just brilliant.'

A head-spinning mix of panic, relief and attraction raced

through her. 'She probably won't use my drawings, though. She just wanted a sample to send to the publisher so they get an idea of how she sees the layout and stuff.'

'What about the paintings? Are you including those?' He glanced up at the wall to where she'd painted some of the same flowers, a mix of detail and dramatic licence.

Never. She could just cope with sending the drawings by thinking of them as being like the anatomical illustrations she'd done as part of her study. That was why her lecturer had rung her. She'd always got bonus points for the detailed drawings she'd done in her laboratory book. They weren't really 'art'.

Oh, who was she kidding? She'd sweated blood on them, pouring her heart in.

She grasped her hands together and squeezed, tensing the muscles to ease their adrenalin burn. She fought the instinct to fly to her room and hide her head under her pillow.

'No.'

'You should. They're awesome.' He smiled. A full beamer that pulled her happiness level to new heights. And yet she wanted him out of there all the more. She didn't want this part of her life opened up to anyone.

But he was asking questions, looking at everything. 'So every flower has a meaning. What did you say I'd be? A tulip?'

She winced. Saw him run down the list. Saw him stop. Saw the smile.

Perfect lover.

He lifted his head and looked her straight in the eye. 'You think so, huh?'

Her anxiety about him seeing her work melted away in the heat of his gaze. When he looked at her like that all she could think about was how much she wanted him. Mesmerised, she wanted to answer. Wanted to say 'maybe' in a sassy, challenging way that might encourage him. But she couldn't peel her tongue from the roof of her mouth.

He tossed the draft onto the table and stepped nearer. 'You want to put it to the test?'

It was what she'd been thinking about all week. Dreaming of. Her body was coiled for action yet her tongue still wouldn't budge.

But something must have given her away because his face lit up, and his smile was small but sensual—just the corners of his mouth teasing upwards. He made another move closer.

'I think we should. Don't you?'

Her lips parted but still no sound came, so she just let her body talk instead, leaning towards him as he took the final step to close the gap. He caught her and pulled her home. Her lashes lowered and she tilted her head, relaxing into his body. But he didn't kiss the mouth she offered. His fingers combed through her hair, sweeping it aside to reveal her neck, and it was there that his warm lips descended. Starting at the ultra-sensitive spot below her ear and slowly slipping down and a little cry escaped her. His arms tightened, his hands warm through the thin fabric of her dress. She wanted to kiss him, taste him, but he was out of reach, kissing her collar-bones while his hands gently rocked her against him. Her head fell back, eyes closing; all she could do was rest against him and let the sweet sensations slide through her.

His lips trailed across her, sparking flames across every painstaking inch he covered. As her breathing accelerated so did her desire and her need for more than this. As if he'd sensed the subtle shift he lifted his head. His hands held her tighter to him. She opened her eyes and took in his flushed features.

'Not pretending any more, Emma. This game's going up a level and we're playing for real now.'

Real, but still playing. Could she handle it? She blinked slowly, knowing he could offer her the night of a lifetime. But that was all it would be. There was going to be nothing permanent about this. He was only here for a few more weeks and anyway he played hard and moved on. She didn't know what would happen later; all she knew was that right now she couldn't stop.

'Yes.'

He expelled a large breath, stepping back, taking her hand, heading straight to her bedroom. Confident, in control and not giving her any chance to change her mind. In the centre of her room he turned to face her and she tingled at his expression, at knowing the desire she saw there was real. He pulled on her hand, drawing her to him like a dancer guiding his partner towards him into an embrace. She lifted her face but he still didn't take her lips. Instead he kissed her face, neck and shoulders, his hands firm as they moved over her body. She heard the swishing sound and realised that her dress had just slipped to the floor and all she now wore was a pair of panties.

He lifted his head and stood back a fraction, his lashes showing long on his cheek as he looked down, down, down the length of her.

As she stood there, exposed to his scrutiny, all her inadequacies came to the fore. It was all right when they kissed, when he touched her. She forgot everything then. But having him stand and look at her that way, all she could think was how she could never measure up to the bevies of blonde beauties she'd mentally attached him to. 'I'm not exactly…'

His lashes swept up, the heat in his eyes lancing her. 'Perfect. You're perfect.'

She didn't believe him, self-conscious as she saw him gaze at her bared breasts. 'I'm not very big.'

'Who needs big?' he muttered. 'All you need is enough to do this…' He stepped forward as he spoke, bending and taking her nipple and the softly swollen flesh around it into his hot mouth. She gasped, her legs losing the ability to support her, and his arms tightened, holding her up as he licked and sucked. Pure want shot through her. He still hadn't kissed her mouth and her desire for that grew desperate. She called to him, whispering his name over and over. She watched from half-closed eyes as he continued to torment her.

He guided her back against the bed, lifted his head, and with a gentle smile that teased he gave her a little push, tumbling her backwards. He followed immediately and they landed together on the mattress. Her insides totally turned to mush as her body took on the weight of him.

With his arms either side of her, enclosing her in his warmth, he finally bent his head to kiss her lips. She met him eagerly and her passion exploded as the depth increased. She held his roughened jaw between her palms, holding him in place as much as he pinned her. The kiss grew crazy. Hot, feverish need made her want to speed things up. Having him braced above her like that, all it made her want to do was part her legs—wide. She wanted him, *all* of him.

Then he moved away and the disappointment was like a kick in the gut. He lay on his side, propping his head on his hand, and that teasing smile had widened. 'Time for some fun, Emma.'

She wasn't sure what he had in mind. The only hint that he was as affected by that shattering kiss was his faint breathlessness. It made her realise this was so much more for her than for him. She was about to baulk when his fingers played a scale down her stomach. The touch set off a symphony of sensation. He bent forward and his mouth followed their trail and down he slid. He slipped his fingers under the waistband of her panties, ran them around the edge, pulling at the elastic. He looked up at her with a smile that was wickedly lusty and so infectious. Heat washed over her, sudden and intense. He wanted it and she wanted him to do it. Now.

He somehow got the message. Maybe it was the impatient flex of her hips towards him. He knelt, slipped her panties off her hips, down her legs and off. He flung them away and turned back to her with an expression of extreme anticipation. He slid his widespread hands firmly from her ankles up her calves to her knees and then thighs, pushing them apart with ease. She lay back, watching him as he looked at her, excitement tightening as the pressure of his fingers increased as did the almost feral glaze in his eye.

'I'm sorry, Emma, I can't wait, I just have to...' And he bent his head and tasted her core, once.

She exhaled, not realising she'd been holding her breath. Should she be embarrassed about how turned on she was? How wet she was?

'Emma.' He lifted up from her. 'You have no idea how

much I want this. Want you like this.' The look he sent her was viciously searing. Then he was back, burying his mouth and tongue into her, like a man starving, a man who couldn't get enough of her flavour. Licking, sucking as he had her breast only this was even more sensational. Gently, then harder, then gentle again, he teased her. He hooked her legs over his shoulders, settling between them, his hands under her buttocks lifting her so she was utterly available to him. And all she could do was lie there and try to absorb the sensations, the delight, and try to stay cognisant. The flush in her cheeks was intolerable and she flung her arms wide across the bed. He was taking control and giving her the freedom to do nothing but feel. The faint abrasiveness of his lightly shadowed jaw tickled her thighs as her tension rose. She wanted the release but she never wanted this torment to end.

Reason tried to claw its way back to the surface, but she was sunk again as he nipped at the tender skin of her inner thighs.

He soothed with his lips. 'Do you like that?'

Her breathing was short and her answer came in a barely audible puff. 'Yes.'

He did it again. 'Keep saying that, Emma. That's all I want to hear you say to me; just keep saying yes.' The strain in his voice excited her more.

'Yes.' Any other response was impossible. Her fingers curled into the bedspread as she tried to control her reaction. But with every caress that control crumbled. Reality slipped away. Her focus slipped away. All she could do was feel him, the heat of his breath, the firm stroke of his tongue, the suck of his lips and the hard grip of his fingers on her hips, keeping her where he wanted, not letting her pull back, but fuelling the journey to ecstasy.

Her breathing turned ragged; another few licks and she was gasping. Her hands lifted and she grasped his hair, whether to push him away or keep him there she wasn't sure.

He lifted his head a millimetre to mutter, 'Don't fight it. I want to taste it. Let me...let me.'

She pushed his head back down and bucked upwards to meet him, crying aloud as he sucked again and again until every muscle in her spasmed. The 'yes' she screamed was barely recognisable. For seconds her body was locked rigid until finally the tension snapped and extreme pleasure washed through her—waves in which her consciousness almost drowned.

She lay, eyes closed, breathing deepening and she felt his finger gently trace through the wetness at the top of her thighs, and then gently slide right into her. Her eyes flew open as desire jerked through her again and she found herself staring into his blazing face. 'Jake.' She didn't care how much of a beg it sounded.

He moved, coming to lie on her, his jeans rough against her skin. His hair mussed from where she'd driven her fingers through it, gripping him as he'd pulled her through the fire. Their eyes met, his stormy and his breathing rough. 'Are you still saying yes to me, Emma?'

She curled her legs around his waist, rubbing against the taut denim. 'Yes.'

'You're ready for me.' Part question, part statement of fact.

'Yes.' Soft and supplicant. No way was there any other answer.

He bent to kiss her and suddenly all that mattered to her was getting his jeans off. He rolled off her, lying on his back as he ripped open the belt and yanked them down.

And then he froze.

She stared. 'What?'

'I don't have a condom.' He swore sharply. 'Please tell me you have some.'

He whipped his head round at her silence. 'Please.'

'You don't have one in your wallet?'

His fingers raked through his hair as he cursed.

She figured he must have forgotten to replace it last time he used it. She pushed away the stray thought. She didn't have any. Had never had the need. Even more embarrassingly, wouldn't know how to put one on. Colour ran high and doubts came flying in. What was she doing?

'No, you don't. Don't go cold on me.' He moved fast, taking her hands in his and pinning them at the sides of her head while he kissed her hard and deep until she was thrusting up against him, that squirming, desperate mass again.

'We both want this. You have no idea how badly *I* want this.' She did. She was the same.

'What about your toolbox? You were the one who said about being prepared.'

'Screwdrivers, yes; condoms, no.'

He moved off to rest beside her and they lay together in frustrated silence.

'What about asking your neighbour?'

She was mortified. 'As if. It's hardly like asking for a cup of sugar, is it?'

He started laughing so hard and she mock-punched him on the arm. He immediately tussled back, flipping over her, pressing against her and suddenly so, so, close—the only thing separating them the strained cotton of his boxers. Their eyes locked.

He suddenly looked as serious as she'd ever seen him. 'I don't have a condom with me because I wasn't expecting this to happen. Not yet anyway.'

'But you did expect it?'

'I've been wanting it to happen all week.'

I've been wanting it to happen for years.

She slumped down in the bed, half in frustration, half in despair at her own desperation. She'd thought she was finally going to get somewhere. He'd wanted her. And now that moment was lost. She pulled at the sheet, wanting to cover her cooling body.

Suddenly he was out of the bed and pulling his jeans back up, struggling big time with the zip.

'Where are you going?'

'The service station. There's one round the corner from the park. I can run, be back in less than ten. Don't move. Do. Not. Move.'

He kissed her again—pressing her down into the mattress, leaving her lips bruised but bursting with pleasure. Then he was gone, pulling the tee shirt over his head as he exited the room. She lay staring after him, and lasted about thirty seconds.

The front door flung open just over ten minutes later. He looked at her and sighed. 'You moved.'

She looked at him and nearly melted on the spot. Every whisper of doubt fled again at the sight of him. His intention was obvious. He puffed slightly, a light sheen of sweat beaded on his brow. He clutched a small box. It wasn't even in a bag.

'Have you changed your mind?'

She couldn't answer vocally, still too unsure, so she shook her head just a fraction.

'Well,' he said with a philosophical tone as he strolled towards her, 'I guess it means I get to undress you all over again.'

She stood still. Didn't run, didn't move towards him. Just stood waiting, wanting. Tipped her head back the second he was in range. Mouth open, damp everywhere.

His arms wrapped around her and he lifted her up. She curled her legs around his waist and he walked through the tiny cottage to her bedroom. All the while their lips sealed, their tongues dancing and their arms locked about each other.

His hand slid up her thigh and he lifted his head and grinned at her as he discovered her lack of underwear. She'd been so wet, still was. Putting panties on would have created unnecessary laundry.

He lowered her to the ground and disposed of the dress. His shoes, jeans and tee rapidly followed and at last the searing contact resumed—full-on, fast, frantic.

He broke his mouth away from hers. 'We have to slow this down.'

'Why?'

His grunt of laughter was muffled against her shoulder and he fell back on the bed, pulling her with him. They landed on the box of condoms he'd tossed down a moment before. He ripped it open and had one on in less than a minute.

He paused and looked at her.

She swallowed hard at the sight of him. At the size of him.

He seemed to sense her nerves. 'Slow, smooth, close.' He echoed the words of the conversation of only last night. It seemed for ever ago.

Dancing with Jake. Already she hoped she would get to do it again. Dangerous territory. But the worrying thoughts vanished—along with all others—as he moved, settling over her. The speed of seconds ago was gone. Instead his actions were gentle, deliberate. His hands held her head. He wouldn't let her break eye contact. Her barely acknowledged fantasy of half a lifetime was about to become reality.

Slowly, smoothly, he got close and she'd never felt so excited. Her eyes widened as her body stretched to take him. She wanted it more than she'd ever wanted anything. She took a deep breath. 'Please don't stop. Please don't stop.'

His fingers came over her mouth. She was silenced by them and by the sudden flare in his eyes. He squeezed them shut. 'Concentrate. I *have* to concentrate.'

She lay still, as did he, for the beautiful moment they became one. His eyes flashed opened again and she saw his pupils huge and glowing. He lifted his fingers away from her mouth, replacing them with his lips. Then he smiled at her.

'Don't worry, I'm not going to stop. We've barely started.'

And then he did start, his hands, mouth and hips working together to cause an overdose of sensitivity in her limbs and soul.

She started too, understanding, giving back. She kissed him, ran the tip of her tongue down his neck to taste him, and used her hands to urge him closer. She couldn't contain the cries of delight. Moving with him to create exquisite sensations until with a harsh groan he reared up onto his hands, arching back above her. The muscles in his arms rippled, his chest golden and broad. He ground against her, driving deeper. The edges of her vision darkened, she could see only him, feel only him. She was hardly aware of her moans, the sounds of pleasure just escaping. Effortless joy.

There was nothing slow about it any more. And it felt fantastic. And suddenly she was gone—he'd sent her to some other galaxy, a state of bliss.

He dropped to his elbows, gathering her to him as her body shook. They couldn't have got closer. She heard his groan and felt the hot way he muttered her name over and over as he powered everything into her.

She lay, laxness seeping into her bones. The weight of him welcome in her lethargy.

'I'm not too heavy, am I? Can you breathe?'

'I'm fine.' Cocooned in his arms, still connected, she was more than fine. She wanted this moment to last for ever.

As soon as she'd thought it the reality struck at her. It wasn't going to be for ever. A trickle of chill flowed into the warmth of a moment before. It became a flood as the madness lifted and cold sanity returned. She'd just slept with Jake Rendel. A life-changing event for her, but she was just another girl for him.

She hoped it had been OK. If it had been half as good for him as it had for her then she was in the clear. She felt tears spring to her eyes and she wriggled underneath him, suddenly needing to step back.

He kissed her ear swiftly and whispered, 'We really need to do that again.'

Yes, but she needed to shore up her defences first. 'I'm just going to nip to the bathroom.'

She slid from the bed and looked for something to wrap around her while he rustled in the bed. She heard his mutter, then she heard his shout.

'Emma!' Startled, she looked at him. 'Why the hell didn't you tell me you were a virgin?'

CHAPTER SEVEN

'DOES it matter?' Emma looked at where he'd pulled back the sheet to where the evidence stared them hard in the face. The look of shock on his face as he computed the info wasn't encouraging.

'Of course it matters. What are you doing giving your virginity to—?' He broke off. His frown deepened. 'I could have hurt you. Did I hurt you?'

'No.' She sighed. 'OK, just a little to start. Then it was, it was…' *Mind blowing*, but she couldn't quite say it. 'I was ready, Jake; you said it yourself.'

With relief she watched him pull the sheet up. It was hard for her to concentrate on the conversation with him lying in all his magnificent naked glory. She'd started to want him all over again—but still wanted that mind space too.

'Why didn't you tell me?'

'Would it have made a difference?' Would you have stopped? She hadn't wanted to run the risk. She'd wanted him too much.

He stared at her darkly as he pondered that one. Then, 'I could have made it better for you.'

Hysterical giggles weren't too far away. Better? Impossible. At least he hadn't said it had been a mistake—yet.

He continued to lecture. 'It should have been more special. Were you waiting for marriage?'

The look of terror that crossed his face as he asked had her determined to straighten him out.

'Jake, stop being so old-fashioned. It had to happen some time. Hell, according to some magazine I read most women kiss twenty-nine men before they get married!'

'Twenty-nine?' He glowered. 'How many have you kissed? What number am I?'

She knew her colour was high and no way was she going to tell him he was her first in all departments. 'What does it matter? And you know what number you are in bed, so you can be pleased about that. I was ready for this to happen and why not with you?' The best form of defence was attack. 'I bet you can't even remember what number I am for you. At least it meant one of us was a pro.'

He sat bolt upright and frowned at her. 'Well, that's charming. Who do you think I am?'

'Well, you said yourself you're a playboy.'

'Ok, I'll be honest. I'm not exactly celibate, but I'm not out on the pull every night either.'

Her scepticism must have been clearly evident.

'I'm not. I have one girlfriend at a time. With a gap in between. We spend time together, have fun, move on. I'm up front. She knows, I know.'

'How long do they usually last?'

'A few weeks.'

'Is that what we're doing?'

Silence. He glowered at her before huffing back down on the bed.

'I don't know what we're doing.' He lay rubbing his hands over his eyes. His forehead creased.

She watched him cautiously. He really didn't seem to be taking this too well. She hadn't thought it would matter that much—or not to him, at least.

Fists clenched, he let out a roar.

She jumped. 'What?'

He flung back the sheet with theatrical panache. 'Look at me. God, I wanted you all over again and now even more so. There are just so many ways we have to do this together. So much I have to show you. You haven't had sex standing up, on top...all kinds of ways.'

She stared at him. Stared at his body. The tension even greater than before, he was the epitome of raw, ready man, muscles bunching, and she knew he was about to pounce. Excitement started to flood out her doubts again. 'So what, now you're going to be my coach?'

'Hell, yes.' He gave a wicked laugh. 'You know, for a beginner you have an outstanding level of natural ability. You're going to be a star pupil.'

'Always am, sir.' She batted her lashes at him. Keep it cool, keep it light. Take advantage of one incredible lover and try not to get your heart smashed in the process. She could handle this. She could. 'OK, but first I have a shower.'

'Not without me, you don't.'

He was out of bed and grabbing a condom from the box before she'd taken a step.

She turned and ran for the bathroom, giggling as he lunged after her. Worries whisked away in the chase.

'Would you believe I'm starving?'

They sat in the kitchen. She'd slipped her dress on again and he lounged in his tee shirt and boxers.

'Yes, because so am I. I've got steak in the freezer, oven chips and mushrooms I can make a sauce with.'

'Anything green?' His eyes twinkled.

She wrinkled her nose. 'Some chopped tomato and a bit of lettuce on the side?'

'You're such a carnivore.'

She smiled.

'Where do you put it all?'

She shrugged. 'Fast metabolism, I guess. I like meat.'

He sliced the mushrooms while she put the chips in the oven and prepared the steak.

'Is it too early for a drink? Got anything to drink?'

'Wine.'

'From home?'

'Of course.'

They carried the plates outside and sat on the verandah again. He'd demolished half his steak when he caught her eye. 'I can't believe you were a virgin.'

She swallowed. 'Why?'

'You're twenty-six.'

'So?'

'You don't think that's a little unusual these days?'

'We're not all at it like rabbits from the age of, what—sixteen?'

The rascally grin appeared. 'You can't tell me you've never been hit on by anyone. What about university?'

'What about it? I was so busy I just didn't have the time.'

'You didn't go to all the start-of-year parties? End-of-year parties? All-year-round all-night-long parties?'

'I studied. If you want to come top you don't go to parties.'

'Emma, I didn't even *go* to university but I still went to the parties.'

'Why am I not surprised?'

'What about the hotel?'

Getting fed up with the conversation, she pushed her plate away. 'Sure I get asked out. They're always much older. They're almost always married.'

He chuckled. 'You're a victim of your own success.'

Success? Hardly. 'What do you mean?'

'You intimidate guys your own age. You probably earn more than most of them. You're incredibly efficient and good at your job. You have them all shaking in their boots. Whereas older men appreciate your power.'

She rolled her eyes. He was just being generous about a pathetic situation. 'You're not that much older than me. You're not intimidated?'

'I earn more than you.' He looked smug.

'And if you didn't?'

He winked. 'You don't scare me, Emma Delaney.'

* * *

It was a complete lie. She terrified him. The last few hours had been the most intense of his life. And his head couldn't quite catch up with it all.

'You won't tell anyone, will you?' She looked anxiously at him.

'What, that you were a virgin?' Who on earth was he going to tell? Ten years ago he probably would have carved it into a tree somewhere, but he was beyond that now—maybe.

She gave a weak smile. 'No. About the room.'

'Your paintings?'

She nodded, not looking at him.

Her worry confused him. 'Why not?'

'I just don't want people knowing. It's nothing.'

'It's not nothing, Emma, they're incredible. You should be proud of them.' He was still in shock about it. In shock about everything. That no one knew about her paintings was astounding; that she'd studied a whole other degree and not told her parents was bizarre. The irony got him. Her father would have been even more proud of that.

'Jake, I really don't want to talk about it. And I don't want you going in there again.'

He looked at her, not sure he could promise either.

'You don't want to talk about it? You must—you never have. Talk to me, at least talk to me.' He didn't want her to shut the door on him on this. Now that he was in, he didn't want to be turfed out.

'There's nothing to say. It's just a hobby, that's all.'

He knew it wasn't. She put hours into it. All those paintings were evidence of that.

'Why don't you show them? You should at least hang some in your house. People would be so interested.'

Her frown got bigger with every word he spoke and he couldn't think why. She had talent—in spades, as usual. Why on earth wouldn't she want to share it?

'I don't want people to be interested.'

She looked like a petulant schoolgirl, but then she bent over her plate and he couldn't help but notice the gentle curve of her breast as her dress slipped. No schoolgirl here; she was all woman. Petite and perfectly formed.

She glanced up and caught the line of his gaze and her lips curved up.

Sexy. Sultry.

Jake blinked. She might not have that much experience but she sure knew how to push his buttons—a single-touch direct-dial to his hotline.

He gripped the cutlery. He'd discovered all of Emma's secrets today. At least he hoped he had all of them. He didn't know if he could handle much more.

Emma gave up on the last of the steak. Being with Jake did dangerous things to her. Her appetite for food seemed to have disappeared. But her hunger for him was growing minute by minute. She was in danger of keeling over from famine any moment. Fainting at his feet would be too uncool.

She wanted him to forget about her paintings. He was never going to understand why she needed it to be hers and hers alone. He hadn't had to deal with the level of expectation she had and wouldn't understand the bliss of being able to do something badly if she wanted. With no one judging. But while she couldn't make him understand, maybe, just maybe, she could distract him. Make him forget. She stood up from the table but couldn't hide the wince.

'Sore?' His voice was low and chocolatey rich.

She felt the colour rise in her cheeks. 'A little.'

He stood and took the plate off her, setting it down on the table. 'Let me see if I can help you loosen up. Ease away the aches and pains.' In a smooth, effortless move she was off her feet and in his arms.

'Jake!' But she didn't mean the indignation. To be carried as if she weighed nothing more than a feather made her feel incredibly feminine.

He headed straight to her bedroom and her blood started pumping.

'I really need to kiss you again, Emma. Everywhere.'

With his arms so firm around her—what could she do but let him?

Some time later she lay, naked, spread-eagled and sated—for the moment. He lay on his side next to her, head propped up on his elbow, grinning at her wickedly.

'Better?'

Much. But she didn't like this one-sided business.

She sat up and leaned over him. Shyly bold. Pushing up his tee shirt and tracing a finger down his chest. Bending over to let her lips follow its path. Down, down, down.

Then he lifted his hand and stopped her.

'No.'

Startled, she looked at him.

'I don't want you to.'

She had that horrid hot-then-cold feeling. 'Why not?' She glanced down for reassurance and got it: the bulge in his boxers was enormous.

'I don't want you to feel you have to.'

'I don't.'

He smoothed his forehead with his fingers. 'You're always doing things for others because you think you're obligated to. I don't want you to feel that way with me.'

'I do not. I'm not.' Why did he think this? Why couldn't he see that she made her own decisions for herself? Inexperience made her feel inadequate. 'Are you scared I'll do it wrong?'

He laughed. 'Honey, there is no wrong.'

She sighed. He had *her* all wrong—didn't he?

He stared at her with eyes that were dark and unfathomable. 'Tell me.'

'What?'

'Tell me why you want to. Prove it's not because you think you have to.'

She froze. Embarrassment washed over her. That was certainly something she'd never done before. Tell him what she really wanted? *Why* she really wanted it? She couldn't remember when she'd last done that in any area of her life. Open up those secret desires? She looked at him and saw the challenge. It's a *game*, she reminded herself, just a game. And she could make up the rules if she wanted to. A smidgeon of confidence at that thought enabled her to answer.

'I'm not doing this because I think you want me to. Hell, it appears you don't. I want to for *me*.' She coughed, tried for a little more volume, but still didn't make it much past a whisper. 'OK, I've never…touched a guy this way. Maybe I'm curious. Maybe I want to learn. Maybe I want to make you feel the way you do me—I want to know I can do that.'

She felt burningly awkward. But then he was the one who said he'd be her coach.

He sat up, took her chin with a light touch and tilted her head so he could kiss her—gently, so sweetly. He lifted his head and stared hard into her eyes. She held the gaze, feeling herself growing more excited by its intensity, feeling her want for him grow even more. Suddenly he pulled the tee shirt over his head. 'If you insist, who am I to stand in the way of a decent education?' His mouth broke into that magnificent smile and she had the urge to just kiss him and climb aboard. But she wanted to discover him first. Inch by glorious inch.

She smiled, shyly excited. 'I *want* to explore you, Jake.'

He lay back, screwing up his eyes. 'I don't think it's going to take much, Emma. This conversation alone just about has me exploding.'

She rose to all fours and bent over him. Just looking at first. Then touching. First with her fingers, then with her tongue.

Her shyness disappeared as experimentation took over to find what would make him shiver, what would make him tense, what would make him groan.

She achieved it all, loving his reactions, and when he suddenly gripped her shoulders she looked up at his face. His eyes were open now, intensely fixed on her actions.

'OK?' she asked.

His head jerked in the affirmative. She figured the flush in his face was a good sign. She bent her head again.

'Emma, Emma, Emma!' His hands slipped under her arms and he pulled her up the bed. 'Please tell me you're not too sore now,' he asked as he frantically donned a condom.

'Not too sore.' She smiled as he pressed onto her.

'You're ready?' His breathing broken.

'Yes.'

CHAPTER EIGHT

At 7:30 A.M. Emma walked into her office and stopped mid-stride halfway across the floor. In her single-stem specimen vase stood a perfect red tulip. She glanced around, half hoping someone was there to witness the biggest smile she'd ever worn at that time of day. No one present. Then she slapped herself. Idiot girl.

She was unable to concentrate on the screen at all; her gaze kept darting to the flower. She wriggled on her seat as she kept re-living parts of the weekend. Not a good idea. Intolerable heat alternated with moments of sheer panic. She had the sinking feeling it had meant a lot more to her than Jake. And more than was good for her, given his record of nil-commitment. But she'd known what she was getting into from the start—some fun. Short-term. He was only in town a few weeks anyway. She was just going to have to get over it.

But that didn't stop her dreaming.

She pushed away her keyboard and pulled out a blank piece of paper. Opening her drawer, she selected a couple of lead pencils. She picked up the specimen vase. She just wasn't going to get any work done till she'd satisfied her creative itch. She studied the flower, carefully touched its silky petals, ran her finger down its strong, smooth stem. It was a magnificent example.

She set it down on her desk and started to draw it.

She marked precise, sure lines on the paper, added curves and shading, and soon the tulip looked back up at her in 2D. She smiled, her tongue poking out the corner of her mouth.

Self-mockery curved the smile further as she thought to add something else. She curled a second stem around the straight stem of the tulip. Then the head of a smaller flower took shape. Her daisy.

Her door opened and she looked up guiltily. Max came towards her. 'How are you getting on with that report?'

She glanced at the clock on her computer—nine a.m. Hell, somehow she'd just wasted over an hour on a doodle.

'It's taking a little longer than I'd expected.'

Mortified, she berated herself. She should have worked on it at home in the weekend. Most certainly she should have been working on it now—in work time! Instead she'd been daydreaming about the boy next door. How pathetic.

Max was looking across the room at her through slightly narrowed eyes. 'You'll have it for me tomorrow though, won't you?'

'Of course.' That meant working hard at it from this minute on. She was not going to lose her concentration—or her career—on a fling. Max turned to leave. She snatched up the sketch and tossed it at the bin. Focus, focus, focus.

'Morning.'

She lifted her head so fast she almost gave herself whiplash.

Jake stood in her doorway, smiling hello and stepping aside for Max as he passed on the way out. Max turned and gave them both a look that Emma was wary of interpreting.

As soon as Max was out the door Jake shut it behind him. Throwing her a wicked look, he turned the lock.

'Ever had sex on your desk?' He laughed. 'Oh, no, of course you haven't.'

'No, and I'm not about to.' But her body thought different. It was already warming up and anticipating the action.

'You don't think?'

She walked backwards, hands out—half defending, half beckoning. 'Jake, no.'

'Jake, yes.' He'd undone the top buttons of his shirt as he walked towards her. She stared at his chest, every carnal thought of the last few hours re-entering her head and priming her body.

'Jake.' Rational thought was slipping away.

His grin was utterly wicked as he stepped closer. 'Jake, yes.'

'Yes.' He was with her now. And she was wrapping around him.

They kissed and then he lifted his head to look at her accusingly. 'You taste of Caramello.'

She laughed. 'Good thing you like it too.'

'Tastes even better mixed with you.' He bent and kissed her again. She pressed into him. The hours apart felt like years and she couldn't wait to feel him again. He'd gone back to his apartment after spending Saturday night with her. A night where they'd put in hours and hours of study together. Study of all things physical and pleasurable in each other. Until she'd been exhausted and he'd declared himself utterly spent. They'd cooked breakfast and then he'd gone. He'd needed to work. She'd needed to work. She had intended to. Instead she'd lain on her sofa on the verandah in the sun and struggled to believe it had all actually happened. If it hadn't been for the all-over body ache she would have thought she'd dreamt it.

Now, twenty-four hours later, he was scrabbling with her shirt and she was frustrated with his seemingly glued-on belt. He lifted his head from her collar-bone and growled. 'You do the buttons because I'm all thumbs and I'm going to rip it off if it's not open soon.'

She lifted her hands and swiftly dealt with them.

'I'll do the skirt.'

She chuckled as he simply pushed it up, dropping to his knees to slide her panties down. He loitered over the task. Her giggles became gasps.

'Jake, take care of the condom.' She could hardly get the words out.

He stood and pulled one out. 'I have one in every pocket now.' It was on in seconds, she was on the desk and he was on her, in her and they were away together. She looked up at him and knew her face mirrored his excited expression.

'I can't believe how good this feels.' He growled in her ear as his hands worked through her hair, messing it from its clasp.

'I know,' she whispered, curling her legs around him and arching up. She couldn't get enough of him. Couldn't get enough of this crazy ride. In the hours apart from him her body's excitement level had been building and it didn't take long to reach explosion point. She grabbed some material of his shirt sleeve between her teeth to stop the screams. She felt him nuzzling and nipping at her neck and knew it was for the same purpose.

Minutes later she floated down from the heights and absorbed the flaming madness of their actions. Since when had she ever acted so crazy? Since when was she so willing to abandon anything and everything for a few lust-fuelled moments? She'd never let her wants overrule her obligations before.

It was then she noticed that her stapler was digging into her back. He pushed away from her, standing up from the desk, and, taking her hand, pulled her to her feet.

Embarrassed, she bent and retrieved her panties from the floor.

'You often have sex at work?' The wildness that had overtaken her was more than a little terrifying.

He pulled his belt though its loop. 'Actually no, this is a first for me too.'

He didn't quite meet her eye, and she could almost believe he was embarrassed too. Surely not.

The phone rang. Eyes wide, she answered, hoping she didn't sound too breathless. Becca. Reminding her of an appointment.

She hung up, desperately pulling her clothes right. 'I'm late for a meeting. I'm never late.' She smoothed down her skirt, thanking the stars it wasn't linen or the creases would be unbelievable. 'Do I look OK?'

* * *

Jake surveyed her and inwardly cringed. Did he tell her? He hadn't meant to do it, but he'd been trying to be quiet and nibbling on her neck had stopped him from letting the shouts of lust out. OK, so he'd done more than nibble, he'd been sucking long and hard like some starving vampire. He couldn't get enough of her. And now she had the love bite to prove it.

It was one thing to touch an arm here, throw a look there and give the impression of an affair to her workmates, it was another to thrust such an obvious mark of passion in their faces. Anyone else and he'd have laughed. But this was Emma and Emma was not tacky and he didn't want to upset her. Then he figured a solution.

'Let your hair out.'

'What?' She put a hand to her hair.

'It's all coming out anyway.' He gestured. 'Sorry.'

She took it out of the clip and shook her head. It tumbled down round her neck. Perfect.

Her face glowed and her eyes sparkled and he'd never seen her so beautiful. And he wanted her again already.

'You go. I'm going to stay and get dressed.'

She hightailed it out of there. He watched, unable to take his eyes from the gentle sway of her hips as she walked. Bad move—very bad. He pulled his shirt together and worked the buttons with terse actions.

You'd think he'd be able to keep away from her for twenty-four hours, but no. Apparently not.

Despite his fondness for fun he was professional and when at work, he worked. He'd never have got as far as he had if he did otherwise. And yet, here he was, first thing Monday morning seeking her out and tumbling her on a table with very few pre-liminaries. He'd just needed to. Needed her. Needed that sweet, warm body wrapped around him, letting him in. He'd needed another of those life-stopping orgasms. Utterly addictive.

He tucked the shirt in. Took a few deep breaths to rebal-ance. He looked at her desk. The tulip made him smile. He'd found out where the commercial flower markets were and had been there before six that morning to see if any growers had any. They hadn't been going to sell him just the one, but had been happy to when he'd given them enough money for several dozen.

Turning to go, he noticed a piece of paper on the floor that had just missed the waste-paper basket. He bent to put it in for her, but stopped as he saw what was on it. One of her drawings. He studied it—two flowers precisely drawn in pencil. The tulip on the table. His heart lifted; she'd liked it. Then the small daisy wrapped around the tulip, their stems intertwining.

His lips twitched. She'd drawn them. Intimate—as they had been only minutes before. An idiotic amount of pleasure surged through him at the knowledge she'd been thinking of him—of them. Then it dampened as he considered—what was she doing throwing it out?

He carefully folded it over, making sure the paper didn't actually crease. Holding it between forefinger and thumb, he exited the room. He strolled to the room assigned to him and the team and spread it flat again, tucked it into a file and put it in his bag. All the while his out-of-control brain worked furiously to figure out a way to get her alone again.

Emma didn't see him the rest of the day—largely because she hid out in her office hiding her face, flashing at the memory of the morning, of the past weekend. He appeared in her doorway at the end of the day. He stood in the open door, not venturing nearer. She looked across to him and excitement raced through every cell. When was this going to burn out?

'I'm done for the day. What about you?'

With regret she gestured to the pile of files on her desk. 'Got a way to go.'

He nodded. 'Come to my place once you're through. I'll cook you dinner—I owe you a couple of meals.'

A couple? Was he thinking breakfast as well?

'Come into my parlour said the spider to the fly,' she murmured.

He looked at her slyly. 'You think I want to eat you all up?'

She kind of hoped so and the newly released sass in her couldn't help the flirty reply. 'Don't you?'

'Oh, yes.'

She was so tempted.

'We can have a barbecue; it's a warm night.'

'You're in an apartment building; where's the barbecue?' A teeny obstacle and she knew it.

'I have a very large, very nice balcony.'

She was about to say OK when he threw in the trump card.

'And I have a prime piece of meat just for you.'

She looked at him sharply but his expression was innocent— it was only her mind in the gutter and the only prime specimen she wanted was him.

She shouldn't, she really shouldn't. 'I have a lot to do on this report. I might be pretty late.'

'I don't care how late you come just so long as you come.'

And she really wanted to. 'OK.'

'Text me when you leave the hotel.'

She nodded, not looking at him again. She needed to focus on the spreadsheet, not the sex on toast standing in her doorway.

It was after nine when she logged off from her computer. She stood, shaking off the stiffness that had settled in from hunching over the machine for so many hours. She picked up her mobile and mentally debated for a nanosecond. There really was no question. She pushed the buttons.

'Coming now.'

She smirked. She was getting as bad at the innuendo as he was.

It was another hot night. The wind stirred her hair as she walked. Maybe that was the source of her folly—the wind that drove people to commit crazy acts and literally sent the dogs barking. She walked into the lobby. The attendant looked at her. 'Ms Delaney?'

Full marks for service.

He summoned the lift for her. 'Just step in and I'll send you up.'

The attendant must have phoned to let Jake know because he was waiting in his open doorway, looking sinful. Long shorts and close-fitting tee, bronzed muscles on display above and below the material. He smiled and her answering one radiated out from deep within.

'Dinner's just cooking. The sooner we eat, the sooner we get down to furthering your education.'

'You've been putting some thought into that, have you?'

'Uh-huh.' He winked at her and her heart accelerated into attack territory. 'But first, we need sustenance. A bar of Caramello isn't going to be enough.'

Good grief. She could hardly walk for the excitement. Blow the main course, bring on the main event.

He led the way into the kitchen. She looked about. It was your typical soulless serviced apartment. A couple of extra prints hung on the wall to try to give it a cosy feel, but it still looked like a hotel room. There was nothing personal of his evident other than some files on the table, and his laptop.

Empty.

Temporary.

She needed to remember that. 'What happened to the barbecue?' she asked, preferring to look outside than at the reminders of his transience. Pain pricking already.

'Too windy up here.'

Out the window, she saw the branches of the trees down in the park waving wildly. She breathed deeply.

'Smells good.'

'Fillet of beef.' He pulled the tray out of the oven. She moved to lean against the bench and watch as he efficiently served up some hassleback potatoes, letting the meat rest. Then he sliced it. It looked beautifully cooked. She snaffled a stray piece from the plate. Melt-in-the-mouth tender.

He winked at her. 'And a token bit of green, just for show.' Using tongs, he placed a few asparagus spears, drizzled with dressing. 'Getting to know you, aren't I?'

She smiled.

They sat and talked—of the hotel, the renovations, the city, the wine from home. Pleasant but meaningless. As far as she was concerned they were stocking up energy and filling in time.

He cleared the plates. She sat back. Main-event time and she could hardly wait, was burning ready.

But he disappeared into the kitchen for a while, eventually coming out with a stainless-steel bowl and a spoon.

'Pudding.' He answered her silent question. 'Caramel chocolate mousse.'

She could almost cope with having to delay being with him for some of that. 'What's in it?'

'Caramello. Cream. Butter.'

She smiled at the richness—of the pudding and his voice. 'Decadent.'

'Very.' He put the entire bowl in front of her and the solitary spoon.

'Aren't you going to have some?'

'Oh, yeah, I'm going to have some.' The way he said it had her on red alert.

His eyes had lit up with that humorous light that had a huge dollop of lust included. Heartbreakingly attractive.

'What aren't you telling me?'

He said nothing. Pulled up the chair next to hers and sat, close. She swivelled in her seat to face him. With his finger he scooped some of the mousse and painted it on her lips. She flicked her tongue to taste both the sweet and him.

He leant close. 'Told you I was going to eat you all up.' And he kissed her. The chocolate goo warmed and tasted divine, as did the pressure of his mouth on hers. She felt him apply more mousse to the hollow between her collar-bones and decided she must have died and gone to heaven.

He pushed her hair out of the way and kissed the side of her neck. 'I'm sorry about this. I didn't mean to.'

'Didn't mean to what?'

He lifted his head and looked at her. 'The mark on your neck.'

She put her hand there, mouthing the 'oh'.

'It's already fading.' Warily he watched her.

She started to laugh. 'Was it obvious?'

He shook his head. 'Not with your hair down.'

'Shame. You couldn't even get a glimpse of it?'

He looked puzzled. 'Maybe if you moved your hair.'

'Wish I'd known, I'd have given them a flash.'

The light in his eye dimmed and he looked away from her.

She put her palm against his jaw and pushed his face back to her, gathering some mousse with the fingers of her other hand. 'Jake, I am going to have to get you back for that.'

'Are you now?'

'Mmm.' She leant forward.

His smile returned.

They lay half under the table, the bowl of mousse on one side, clothes all around. He kissed away another smear from her belly. 'Why is it that the things that are so bad for us always feel so good?'

Like the creamy chocolate? *Like him.*

'Everything is OK in moderation, I guess.' She swirled her finger in the mousse and licked it off.

'I don't do moderation.' He paused and blew warm air across her chocolate-daubed nipple. 'And neither do you.'

She arched up as he took her into his mouth. He was right—he worked hard, he played hard. And she? She just worked hard. And ate chocolate, lots of chocolate.

And there was nothing moderate about how he made her feel.

The first thing she saw as she opened her eyes was his suitcase standing next to the wardrobe. It reminded her there was nothing serious about this either. He didn't do serious—had told her that from the start. All this could be was a fierce affair for a few weeks and then he'd move on.

But the way she felt right now, she didn't know if she'd ever be able to.

CHAPTER NINE

CUP DAY. Punters and partiers descended on the city to go to the races. Emma mentally harangued Max, who thought it would be fine to refurbish the hotel in the middle of Carnival week when they were fully booked. But the vibe from the street was invigorating, giving her a much needed energy boost. She was living on adrenalin, Jake and chocolate. The hotel was full and it was all hands to the deck. Although that didn't mean the staff weren't determined to enjoy it.

'You want to go in the office sweepstake, Emma?'

Emma paused; she'd never been asked before. Becca was actually smiling at her—well, a slightly knife-like smile, but a smile nonetheless.

'Umm, OK.'

'I have a list of the entrants here.'

Cynically Emma noted how Becca seemed to find it difficult to get spreadsheet data for her when she requested it, yet she could whip up a complex sheet capable of figuring payouts for trifectas and quinellas in no time. But she refrained from commenting.

She heard Jake come into the reception—her sensors acute at detecting his presence. He came and stood beside her. 'Can I play too?'

'You're always playing, Jake,' Emma said blandly, before shooting him a sideways glance, encountering his to her. They swapped smirks.

He studied the sheet.

'Oh, look, this horse is called Foxy Lady—you should definitely pick that one, Emma.'

She threw him an evil look. 'Do they have one called Complete Clown for you?'

'Ouch.' He looked at Becca and winked. 'You know, she's gonna break my heart.'

Emma's skin prickled, knowing it wasn't *his* heart in danger.

At three p.m. they all congregated in the small bar off the lobby to watch the race.

Jake walked in and sidled up next to her. 'You know, we could bet with something other than money.'

'What were you thinking of?' She forced her concentration on the big screen, not on what she wanted to do with the hunk next to her.

'Hmm. My horse wins, you're on top. Your horse wins, you're on top.'

The laughter burst out of her and several staff turned to glance at them.

Jake's horse won.

'Lady Luck is on my side.' He gave her a saucy glance and she felt her cheeks heat. On top. Nice idea.

'Are you going to come out with us tonight?' Emma supposed Becca was asking them both, but it was Jake she stared at.

Jake's lazy gaze flickered over the blonde receptionist and in a moment of pique Emma wondered if her presence was still actually noticed. Then he looked at her and winked. 'Sure thing, eh, Emma?'

'Sure.' It was the last thing she felt like. She just wanted to go home and have Jake all to herself.

Instead, once she'd logged off and Jake had returned from a meeting they joined the masses out enjoying the crazy wind and warm night. The city was alive with people everywhere dressed to the nines.

'I'm hardly going to win best-dressed tonight, am I?' She frowned down at her black suit and white shirt combo. It was hardly going to compete with the stylish ensembles that some of these women had planned for months in advance so they could stand in the Birdcage at the races and be judged. Even those not competing wore stunning dresses with their perfect tans and hair. Emma was so pale even with fake tan on she still looked as if she were made of milk.

'Oh, I don't know. I've kinda got used to the sexy schoolmarm look. I like being the only one who knows the damn sexy underwear you have going on under the knee-length skirts and plain tops. Or lack of underwear,' he teased.

He always knew the right thing to say to make her feel good. Feel attractive. No wonder he was never for long without a girlfriend. His practised charm would have them queuing up. That combined with his good looks and overflowing bank balance. Mr Popular—never single for long.

The buzz his comment had given her disappeared.

They went back to the same bar where they'd met again. Jake couldn't believe it had been less than a fortnight ago. Couldn't believe he had only three weeks to go. He pushed that one to the back of his mind. Instead he watched her. Watched her fight to maintain conversation with the women from the hotel. She clearly didn't feel comfortable in these group situations. Centre stage was not her thing. She'd rather be sitting at her table at home working on her art, or talking shop with Max. He could relate. At times he found all the obligatory corporate events tiresome. Often there was nothing he'd like more than to be in his offices. Or just be home and working with some wood, as he had as a kid with his grandfather. There was something peaceful about it. Like her, he enjoyed creating—but his was nothing on the scale of hers.

Right now he couldn't be bothered being in the bar at all. He just wanted to be in bed with Emma, making the most of it before it faded. It always did fade, this crazy rush of exhilaration—the delight of physical closeness and fulfillment. Admittedly, though, this was extreme. He felt almost desperate for her company. But they were on a time limit anyway. And given the way she distracted him from his work, this was a good thing.

She looked as eager to leave as he felt. He winked at her when she caught his eye and he saw her melt, saw her sparkle back. It made him want her even more. He'd always had the ability to make a joke, make people laugh—even if it was at his own expense. But he'd never enjoyed being able to do it as much as he did with her. He loved to make her smile, to see her soften, and most of all he loved it when she came right back at him with corny lines of her own.

She went to the bathroom and he kept a watch for her return. He met her halfway across the bar. He couldn't keep his distance any longer.

'Come here and kiss me.'

'Gosh, Jake, what happened to your rules?' Her smile was as wide as it got.

'Screw the rules.'

'You want to screw the *rules*?' She paused. 'Or?'

'Or?' He looked at her face on. Turned on as he saw she was relaxed and confident and letting her flirty self loose. 'Are you about to start talking dirty to me?'

'What if I am?' She tossed her head back and raised her brows at him, hamming it up.

He reached for her, pulling her to him. 'You just go for it, honey. Say your worst.' He wished she would. He wanted into her mind as much as her body.

But she giggled and said nothing, inviting him to make better use of her mouth.

He heard the wolf-whistles and managed to lift his head before things got too crazy. 'We've been here before, Emma— enough of a floorshow already.' So much for not being centre stage. He waved a hand in farewell at the hotel staff and led her out of the bar. Her crimson cheeks brought relief to the unexpected knot of anxiety in his chest. He didn't want that kiss to have only been for show.

They walked to her place, passing throngs of people intent

on having a good time. He intended to have a good time too and he didn't need them to do it. His good time was walking right beside him.

'I'm in need of a snack—you?'

He wanted more than a snack. But he didn't mind waiting for a bit. He liked to think it meant he did have some control over his ravenous lust for her. 'All-day breakfast?'

He was rewarded with a kiss.

She pushed away and went to the fridge to get the eggs and bacon.

He opened the freezer to hunt out the hash browns and laughed. At least ten bars of Caramello stood in a stack smack bang in the middle of the shelf.

'What's with the chocolate in the freezer?'

'It goes funny in the fridge.'

He snapped off a piece from the opened packet on the top, popping it in his mouth and slamming the door shut. He moved to steal another kiss as she stood by the pan.

'Now you're the one tasting of Caramello.'

'Had some of your freezer supply. That OK?'

'Perfect.'

The sizzle in the pan was nothing on the sizzle between them. Water on hot oil, the heat spitting in all directions.

They ate standing up, fully aware it was nothing more than a pit stop—a moment to get some fuel in before the endurance rally started. He for one was primed and he had the feeling her engine was revving too. But there was something else he wanted from this evening.

He took his opportunity when she went to shower and change—only just winning over the desire to join her there. He fobbed off her look of surprise by saying he'd do the dishes while she was in the bathroom.

He wanted to check out the room again. He'd ensured he'd charged his phone enough to be able to take a few pictures and maybe even a video. He could email it through in the morning. She might say she didn't want anyone to know, but he didn't buy that.

Why was she producing pieces for a possible publication if she didn't want people to see her work and know it was hers? He could help her. He had contacts. And he, as always, had a game plan.

The curtains were drawn so he flipped on the light. He figured he had a good fifteen minutes. If he knew anything, he knew women took their time in the shower—even ones as lacking in vanity as Emma.

He ruffled through the manuscript, made a mental note of a few of the flowers and their definitions. Then he took some footage of his favourite paintings.

He heard her footsteps and put his phone in his pocket.

'I thought I told you not to come in here.' She wore a robe, her hair damp around her face, her eyes challenging him. 'Don't you know the story of Bluebeard? Curiosity? Cats? You'll get in trouble.'

From the look on her face he had the feeling the trouble might not be that bad. 'What are you going to do? Punish me?' He grinned wickedly. What would his sweet siren do about that challenge?

She picked it up and ran with it in a way he'd hardly dreamed of. 'Absolutely.' She turned and closed the door behind her. Then he heard the sound of a key turning. She spun round to face him. 'You're locked in here now. This is my room, my secret, my fantasy. You want to be a part of it? Then you have to do as I say.'

His mouth went dry. Her fantasy? 'Sure.' He choked the word out.

For a second she hesitated. Then she crossed the room to stand right in front of him. He itched to pull her that inch closer. 'Go and sit by the window.'

He did as she said, no question. Sitting down, he watched as she rearranged things to her liking. She took the drop cloths and spread them, piling them on top of each other to create a large cushioned area.

His body signalled its approval of her actions. Of her robe as it gaped slightly as she bent to her task. But this was her room, her idea and he wasn't going to interrupt. She was opening up to him fully at last.

She picked up the vase of flowers, taking each stem out carefully one by one and placing them around the pillowy sheets. Gently shaking each flower as she lifted it, spreading the scent. He watched, rapt, as she moved with gentle grace, and precision—just as she moved with him. As her picture unfolded he felt himself falling deeper and deeper. And the lust kept the panic at bay.

Emma stood and with a degree of nerves turned to look at Jake. She'd been so engrossed in creating her tableau she'd forgotten that he was here in the flesh, and not just in her dreams. Reality intruded and embarrassment rose. He must think she was an idiot. He sat silently, his eyes huge blue pools, and his focus travelled down her, taking in the scene she'd set and her in the heart of it. Then he spoke, his voice soft but slightly raspy as it broke into the silence of the room. 'Your fantasy.'

She had lost her tongue and just nodded.

Carefully, without breaking the eye contact, he rose and walked across to where she stood at the edge of the floral bed she'd created.

'What do you want me to do?'

Her mouth was dry, making speech seem impossible.

His intent look didn't lift.

She'd totally lost her nerve.

'You started this, you have to say what you want. Tell me.' He leant forward and whispered in her ear. 'If you don't ask, you don't get.'

Her eyes half closed. 'Take your clothes off.'

His tee shirt flew over his head and was tossed into the corner in a second. He stood and looked at her.

She looked back and as she took in his broad chest her confidence picked up. 'All of them.'

He scuffed his sneakers and socks off, kicking them into the corner after the shirt. His hands went to his belt. His jeans were under so much strain it was almost impossible to get the zipper down. She couldn't take her eyes from them and felt the ripening as he yanked them down to reveal his boxers. He slipped them down too and his body sprang upwards, freed from the tight material.

She stared. He really was magnificent. She walked around him marvelling at the perfection of his body. Feeling bold enough to reach out a finger and trace the indents of muscles on his back, his skin warm and smooth.

She came to stand in front of him again. Stared up at his motionless face, the intensity in his blue eyes trapping her.

She lost her tongue again—aching for him to touch her. Why couldn't he? He knew exactly how to touch her—what was he waiting for?

He grinned, seemingly able to read her mind. 'How am I to know what to do for you unless you tell me?'

'You already know; you've already done it.'

His smile broadened. 'You don't need to be shy around me any more, Emma. There isn't a part of your body I don't know. Let me into your mind as well. I want to know your fantasies. I want to *be* your fantasy.'

He already was.

'Will it help if I tell you what I want?' Her stomach tightened at the sound of his voice dropping to that low whisper. 'I want to touch you here.' He gestured to her belly. 'I want to taste you here.' He gestured lower. 'I want to play with your nipples; I want to see them harden even more as you get excited. And I want to hear your cry when I move into you.'

The fire of embarrassment in her cheeks flamed anew with desire. She let her robe drop to the floor.

The corners of his eyes crinkled as he saw her reaction. He was encouraging her to be bold, and he was succeeding. 'Fun, Emma. Tell me. It'll be fun.'

He was right. After all, the whole thing was a game. It didn't really matter. She could do anything, ask anything. 'I want you underneath me.' She wanted to feel his strength between her legs. Wanted to be on top of all that power. She wanted to master his body as he had mastered hers.

He lay down on the makeshift mattress. She knelt, one leg either side of his muscular thighs, and took in the view spread before her. His hard, flat stomach, his golden tanned chest fanning out to broad shoulders. She lifted her gaze to his face; he was looking as serious as she felt.

She picked up one of the violets and shook it over his chest, sprinkling scent and dewy droplets on to it. She traced her finger where the water had landed, tossing the flower in favour of him and him alone.

'Do you want me to move or do you want to set the pace?' His body was taut and anticipation glowed in his eyes.

'Let me.' She inched higher to sit at the apex of his thighs.

He smiled and she played, pressing her body against his. Enjoying the freedom to feel his harnessed strength. She knew his potency, knew that if he let it loose she would be sunk, an unthinking mass only capable of feeling. This time she was enjoying the conscious experimentation. Wanted to see how far she could push him, could push herself.

The energy of restraint rolled off him. She moved closer, kissing him with her mouth, then with her most intimate part—gently rubbing, half sliding onto him before slipping away again. His hands rested on her bottom, not guiding, not trying to control the direction she took, but squeezing slightly, just letting her know he was there and that he was letting her take the lead.

For a few moments.

Then they squeezed harder, became more authoritative, wanting her to take him. She wiggled away and shook her head. He sighed. 'Emma, I can't handle much more.' Tension furrowed his brow, sweat beaded on his chest.

She smiled, the vixen in her finding her power, and she relentlessly continued.

He expelled a harsh gust of air. 'You're playing with me.'

'Yes.'

A grunt of laughter and he conceded defeat. 'OK, I'm happy for you to play with me.'

She continued working, her hips teasing as she slid home, her hands toying with his nipples, then toying with her own, and she watched with satisfaction as he almost lost it.

'Emma.' His head was back on the sheets, his eyebrows pulled together and his eyes shut tight as he so obviously fought to keep control.

It was then she tossed her head back and laughed delightedly. Awareness of her own power dawned on her.

His eyes shot open. 'Oh, I am so going to get you for this.'

'I do hope so,' she answered playfully.

He smiled at her then. And she smiled back, a smile that reflected her realisation of just how much fun this was. How good this felt. He was right—it was fun. She'd shared one of her deepest desires and he'd made it happen for her.

And then he surprised her by swiftly sitting up. The shift brought him even deeper into her. She gasped. He looped his arms around her, holding her tightly to him so their chests were sealed. Their warm bodies combining to create a blazing heat. And in a split-second he reduced her to that shaking mass again, only able to enjoy the sensations he created as he rocked against her. The friction it caused at her nub was unbearably arousing and her head fell back as she moved with him to get closer, ever closer. He kissed the length of her neck, muttering half-sentences she hardly heard.

After, he carefully lifted her off, cradling her beside him. And then he picked up one of the violets, trailing it across her body, the petals cool on her hot skin, beautifully scented. And with a smile he took her fantasy and extended it, making it better than she'd ever imagined. The ecstasy he gave to her was the most addictive drug and she didn't know how she was ever going to give it up.

When she woke she found he'd won the race back to consciousness. He'd pulled back the curtains and the early-morning light flooded the room. It was her favourite time to paint—the quietness of the street, the freshness of the sun's glow. He stood, unashamedly naked, surveying her paintings. She surveyed him.

After last night there were no secrets any more. She knew she could tell him anything. Ask him anything.

She could trust him.

And, oh, boy was her heart going to get mangled when he went back north. But it was far, far too late to pull back. She couldn't say no to him. Couldn't say no to herself.

'These really are fantastic, Emma.'

'I'm glad you like them.' The only person she'd shared her body with and the only person she'd shared her art with. And she'd never regret it.

CHAPTER TEN

'I HAVE to go back to Auckland for a few days. Flying out in an hour.' Jake put his bag at his feet. Emma's face fell and as a result his out-of-control, irritated heart lifted. He walked over to her and she came round from behind her desk, lifting her mouth for his kiss. It was dangerously exciting to be able to have her, even just for a kiss, at any given moment.

She rested her head on his chest. 'I'm so comfortable with you.' She'd spoken softly and he only just caught the words.

Comfortable. For some reason it really rankled. Like an old cardigan you just wore around the house. He didn't feel comfortable with her. In fact, the more time he spent with her, the less comfortable he became. He felt challenged. Physically and mentally.

Emotionally.

And he didn't like it.

He pulled out of her arms, managing a tight smile. 'See you when I get back.'

He turned away from the confusion that sprang in her features, telling himself he was glad he had to go to Auckland. He really needed to get his laidback mojo back. He liked the carefree nature of his relationships—easy come, easy go. But he felt an insatiable intensity with Emma. An uncontrollable need to seek her out. Be with her. He needed to get on top of it. Going home would help because when he was in the same city as her, he just couldn't keep away.

* * *

Emma sat at her desk and stared blankly at her computer screen. Then she shook her head, determined to clear out the dreaminess. She was not going to sit here and moon over his absence. Certainly not going to wonder what he was doing with his time—with his nights. She put her head down, willing herself to get on with it. She'd developed a legendary ability to focus and she needed all of it now.

She spent the latter part of the afternoon in meetings—a helpful distraction from the melancholic awareness that she'd be sleeping alone tonight. On her return to her office she stopped, another surprise on her desk. The tulip still stood in her vase, its bloom widening slightly with age, but tucked in beside it was a tiny blue flower—a forget-me-not. She didn't know how he'd done it. But he had. Underneath his easygoing, jokey nature lay a core of iron. When Jake wanted something, he got it. Including her. For as long as he wanted.

Thursday morning Jake gave instructions to his PA, snapped his phone shut and frowned as he headed towards the building site. He felt off. Definitely a case of wrong-side-of-bed-itis. Or maybe it was a case of alone-in-the-bed-itis. There was a cure. His frown deepened. He couldn't stop thinking about her and this was not a good sign. He was screwing up here and he knew it. Emma Delaney was a good girl. She always had been. And here he was, self-proclaimed commitment-phobe. He'd shouldered enough responsibility in the early part of his life to last him the rest of it. He loved his mother and sister to bits and would do anything for them, but that was enough. He didn't need a serious girlfriend or—heaven help him—wife and kids. He just wanted to have fun. And the women he went with were the same. While Emma might say she was up to the game, it didn't feel right. So he should quit it now. But he couldn't. The dilemma tossed his insides in turmoil.

He looked over at the newsagent's and read the placard advertising the lead story in the day's paper. Despite his brain telling him one thing, his libido was telling him another and this idea was brilliant. His moment of guilt instantly shoved to the side.

Not long into the afternoon of the slow-motion day, Emma took a call from Becca on Reception—'I have a courier parcel here for you. Do you want me to bring it up?'

'No, thank you. I'll come and get it myself.' She needed to stretch out. Use some muscles. Other muscles were begging to be used again, but that wasn't about to happen soon. She wished they'd go back into dormant mode; it made life less difficult.

The slim package bore Jake's company logo in the sender box. She glanced at Becca, who was watching with interest. She gave her a small smile and turned away, managing to make it into the lift before ripping the parcel open.

An airplane ticket and a hastily scrawled note. 'Come with comfortable walking shoes, I have a surprise for you—Jake.'

She read the details on the ticket—flying to Auckland on Saturday morning and back Sunday afternoon. She leaned against the wall of the lift. She needed to finish the last of the drawings for Margaret and get them to her by next Wednesday. She had another raft of data to analyse and prepare for Max. Enough of a workload for three people—she'd need all weekend to try to get on top of it.

She read the note again. No please, no negotiation—but no way could she say no.

Friday was the longest day she'd ever had at work. He'd texted her—confirmed she'd got the parcel, confirmed she was going to board the plane. She hardly slept that night. Mocking herself for being like a kid on Christmas Eve, she tried to work in her art room but it held too many hot memories and she had as much chance of concentrating as a dog being told to sit and stay when a juicy bone was merely a bound away. In the end she sat with wine and chocolate and late-night TV.

* * *

He was waiting by the arrival gate, gorgeous as ever. She vaguely took in the fit body clad in usual jeans and tee, but she couldn't look away from the smile in his face and the heat in his eyes. The kiss was wild.

Both breathless, he pulled away. 'Rules. We have to stick to the rules.'

He took her carry-on case. 'Anyway, I have a surprise for you.'

She giggled at his steely grey convertible. 'Jake, you're a show-off.'

He winked at her. 'Boys and their toys, Emma. You know how it is.'

She sure did. She knew full well she was his current plaything. And that was OK. Sure it was. She was grown-up—she could cope with the game.

He drove out of the airport and turned away from Auckland city, heading towards Manukau instead. She looked at him in query.

'Surprise, remember?'

The traffic was heavy even by Auckland standards. Then they passed a sign—'Ellerslie International Flower Show'. She looked at Jake again and caught him grinning at her.

'Really?'

'Sure.'

Her smile blossomed.

They passed a marshal directing people to parking spots. Jake flashed a piece of paper at him and they were waved through to the front.

Emma raised a brow at him.

'Contacts, darling, contacts,' Jake drawled. 'I forgot it was this week,' he added, 'and it's perfect for you.'

She looked at him and couldn't keep back the glow in her heart. 'Thank you.'

He looked at her and smiled and she wished time would stand still because in that very moment she was happier than she'd been in her life. He was totally focussed on her, on doing something nice for her, and she ignored the fact that he was a player used to spoiling his women. She just imagined it was all for real. For ever.

Or at least for today.

But she knew she was looking through a prism, not seeing reality, but a beautiful version of it.

He reached out and stroked her pony-tail, a soft smile tugging at his mouth.

She broke the spell by looking away. She had to keep just a part of herself back or she was going to end up seriously squashed.

They joined the throng at the entrance gates. Jake relaxed and walked beside her, laughing as her enthusiasm bubbled over.

'I can't believe you got tickets. This is awesome. I've wanted to come but never got round to it.'

Ellerslie: New Zealand's premier flower show and Aotearoa's version of London's Chelsea Flower Show. Design and beauty to the fore. Most of all it was a fun day with crowds turning up to take it all in, picnic and be convivial.

They stood in one of the stalls where visitors could purchase plants to take home. She followed as he walked through the displays.

'Look at that one.' He stopped by a delphinium. He looked at her; it matched the colour of her top perfectly. 'You are *not* a daisy.'

She grinned. 'Yes, I am.'

'You're not common; you're like one of these exotic-looking things.' He pointed out the pink-tinged white petals of a moth orchid.

'Not an ordinary garden daisy, but another.' She looked about and soon spotted the one she meant. She picked up the pot and held it out to him. He looked at the small reddish-brown flower with scepticism.

'Smell it,' she instructed, waving it towards his nose.

He bent and sniffed. 'That smells like…'

'Chocolate. Perfect, isn't it?'

'That's amazing.' He smelt it again and laughed. 'Only you would find a flower that smells like chocolate.'

'Chocolate cosmos daisy. Sweet, isn't it?'

'Very.' He looked at her rather than the flower. 'So what does it mean?'

She frowned. 'Did you have to ask?'

'Yes. Tell me.'

She sighed, putting the flower down and turning away. 'Daisies usually mean innocence.'

He laughed even louder and reached for her. Ignoring the fact they were in a crowded tent in the middle of the morning, she leant into him. His lips came within a hair's breadth of hers.

Then she fluttered her lashes at him and gave him a coy look. 'Rules, Jake.'

He let her slip out of his grasp. 'Honey, you're not that innocent. Not any more.'

She waggled her hips at him as she walked ahead. 'Come on, let's go see the winners.'

They headed out to the large display gardens, looking for the medallists. He took her hand. She told herself it was just so they wouldn't be separated in the crowds. Trouble was, she increasingly felt as if she didn't want to be separated from him at all. He was too much fun to be around.

After almost three hours she was in serious need of sustenance. They headed to the little lake that was surrounded by stalls selling tempting food and crafts.

He seemed to know she was flagging. 'I'll get something; you sit and save a spot.'

She sat in the shade, watched him as he moved from stall to stall, clearly deciding which would provide the best fodder. He moved with lion-like fluidity. Long legs striding out casually, but hinting at the strength and speed available should he set his mind to it. She knew how strong he could be, knew how well defined the muscles covered by the tee were. Her body flared at the memories. She was having a wonderful time, but the need to get Jake alone and out of public view was becoming insistent.

He came back carefully balancing a plate and two filled glasses.

He flashed a victorious smile. 'Found a place with French cutlets.'

She laughed as she saw the stack of them. He offered her one of the glasses and then sat next to her. The plate between them, they sat cross-legged and gnawed on the delicately flavoured chops and sipped the wine, listening to the jazz band in the distance playing mellow tunes. They reached for the last cutlet at the same time.

'It's yours.' He laughed, holding his hands up in surrender. 'I saw a Danish ice-cream place just over there.'

She ate the last cutlet with relish. 'Jake, you know exactly how to please me.'

The atmosphere thickened as their eyes met. She put the cutlet bone down, forgetting it in the sudden heat.

He leaned towards her, whispering, 'You know how I wish I could please you right now?'

'How?'

His eyes flashed. 'I'd lie back on the grass, have you straddle me... Why aren't you wearing a skirt? You should be wearing a skirt, because I'd slide my—'

She needed him to stop. She placed her hand over his mouth. 'Jake, don't torture me.'

He nibbled on her fingers. 'Why not? You've been torturing me all day walking around in your tight jeans, wiggling your hips—'

'Jake Rendel! I didn't ever think I'd see you here. Didn't think flowers were your thing at all. You never once gave me one.'

Emma jerked her hand away. The clanging tones of the intruder buzzed in her ears. Her fingers suddenly feeling cold after the warmth of his soft kisses. She looked up and took in the vision standing in front of them.

The creature gave a little pout and laughed, a silvery, tinkling sound. Flat stomach, slim hips, large bust, long blonde hair. An up-to-the-minute dress that clung to her curves. If she wasn't a model, she should be. Type-A model for Jake. The sinking feeling clawed at Emma, pulling her down. The woman oozed confidence. Someone so sure of her worth that she had no compunction about interrupting a couple obviously involved in an intimate moment.

Jake didn't look remotely flustered as he lazed on the grass. 'Emma, Carolina. Carolina, Emma.'

Emma smiled politely and suffered in silence as Carolina gave her the once-over. She knew she was sizing her up as the competition and was sure she didn't stack up. Saw her take in her navy silk top that had a simple shoestring halter-neck tie.

'Emma likes flowers,' Jake said simply, giving the Carolina woman an indolent smile.

'Oh,' said Carolina. 'Lucky Emma.' She gave Emma another look and then focussed on Jake. 'Haven't seen you around lately, Jake. Where have you been hiding?'

'Christchurch, on a job. Working with Emma, actually.'

'Oh.' She visibly preened. 'Well, give me a call when you can. I'm always up for a night out.'

I'll bet. Emma took a quick sip of her drink to stop herself saying something catty.

Jake just smiled and said nothing very much. Emma no longer wanted to listen. If Carolina hadn't got flowers, Emma wondered what he had given her. Done for her. He might not be serious, but he was a generous and thoughtful lover.

She sat quiet as they said their goodbyes. She was not going to let it cast a shadow over the day, but meeting Carolina opened old insecurities. Emma was nothing like Jake's usual girls. He wouldn't even have been interested if it weren't for the fact he'd felt sorry for her, if she hadn't practically thrown herself at him in the bar, looking for someone to rescue her from her frigid-spinster image.

Jake watched Carolina walk away and wondered why on earth he'd ever dated her. Pretty—sure. Nice—sure. Knew how to party—sure. But she was nothing on the woman beside him now. He'd wanted to take Emma straight home from the airport and have his wicked way with her as soon as possible. He'd fought it. He liked her, liked her company, walking and talking with her, and he'd wanted to be with her as she walked around Ellerslie. He'd be damned if he was going to give in to his body's demands and do nothing but be in bed with her at every opportunity. She deserved more than that. They both did.

He had a need to get to know her better, in her head as well as her body. And it had been fun, lots of fun. She'd shown him how to look closely at the plants—something he'd never bothered with before. She was full of interesting facts and they'd discovered they preferred the same designs. He still could hardly wait to get alone with her, but just being with her was enough for now.

He reluctantly glanced at her. She'd know, of course. No hiding the fact Carolina was an ex—Carolina couldn't have made it plainer. Or that she'd be open to resuming a relationship. It bothered Jake, but, worse, he wanted to know if it bothered Emma. Childishly he couldn't help hoping she would feel jealous. Which was stupid because this was just another of his freeform affairs that would come to its natural conclusion when he did return to Auckland for good. But the thought of her with another man made the reddest mist swirl in front of him and he suddenly ached to know if this was like that for her too.

She was watching Carolina depart. She smiled blandly at him. Her eyes were veiled. It was as if she'd drawn the blinds so she could see out but no one could see in, least of all him. Now he really needed to be alone with her, because when they were alone together she opened up to him and that was what he wanted.

'Let's get that ice cream and get out of here.'

As they walked through the displays he took her hand loosely in his, restraining the urge to grip it tightly. He had the crazy urge to haul her close and tell her how utterly meaningless every relationship he'd ever had had been. A damn stupid thing to want to do—hell, she probably couldn't care less.

They got back into the car and joined the snaking line heading back to Auckland city.

'Where are we going?' She sounded perky. He felt lower.

'I want to show you my apartment.' He was just about fit to burst. He wanted to see what she thought of his place. He didn't share it with many—usually preferring to overnight at his current girlfriend's house rather than his. That way he still had his space—distance and privacy. But he had surprises of his own he wanted to show Emma. And he still wanted it to matter.

The drive took a little longer than usual and she seemed content to let the wind blow through her hair and watch Auckland skate by. His apartment was smack bang in the middle of town. One of the newer high-rise buildings, it boasted floor-to-ceiling windows showing magnificent views across the city to the water. But it wasn't that view that stopped her in her tracks. She stared at the walls.

'Is that a McCahon?'

She stared at him and he knew she was blown away. He smiled. 'Yeah. Do you like it?'

'It's not a print?' she answered herself, shaking her head.

He watched as she slowly moved to inspect the next painting, then the next.

'You collect art.' She didn't sound as pleased as he'd hoped she might.

He stepped after her. 'It's not a huge collection, just a few pieces that I really like.'

A few pieces. More like several that were worth a small fortune, but despite his joking manner he wasn't usually one to brag. They were all Australasian artists. 'A friend of mine runs a contemporary gallery in the city. She keeps an eye out for me.'

He watched for her reaction. Would she be interested? But the bland, veiled look was back and he had no idea what she was thinking. It certainly wasn't the open delight she'd shown when they'd arrived at the floral festival. He was going to have to tread carefully. But he was still going to tread. He still couldn't see why she was so secretive about her work.

Then his attention was caught, again, by the sway of her body as she moved around the room. She looked stunning in jeans and a top that revealed a fantastic portion of her back—her pale skin calling for him to touch. He forced himself to focus—ask the basics and hope for the answer he wanted.

'Want to go out to eat or stay in? I had thought about Sky City, but maybe we could just scale the heights here instead?' He waggled his eyebrows outrageously so she'd laugh at the innuendo and pick the latter.

She stepped out of his reach, only a hint of a smile on her face. 'Actually, do you mind if we go out? I haven't hit Auckland in a while.'

Surprised, he tried to mask the disappointment and came up with another offer. 'Sure. Shall we shower and change first?'

She nodded. 'Do you have a guest bathroom?'

The disappointment was a stabbing pain this time. 'Sure.' Why was she holding him at arm's length? Why more interested in seeing some restaurant than seeing him? It niggled—was it heading for the end already? Not if he could help it.

She paused, looking at one of his wooden sculptures. 'This is nice.'

Pleasure surged through him.

'You mind?' At the shake of his head she reached for it, her fingers running over the smooth wood. Then she glanced around and saw some of the others. The hand-carved fruit bowl, the block off an old rimu fencepost that had simply been polished on one side, the rest left natural. Understanding dawned. 'You made these.' She studied the carvings on the fruit bowl. 'They're really good.'

'They're not.' He laughed. 'I used to like whittling a bit of wood. Picked it up from the old man.'

His grandfather had been able to make anything from wood. Had used to enthral Sienna with little dolls he'd been able to conjure out of any old stick. Jake hadn't made anything for ages but there was something relaxing about taking a piece of natural beauty and making something more out of it. Slowly carving out something special. But where he was a tinkerer, Emma was a professional—or she could be. Her fingers stroked the wood again and he watched as she then curled them away.

* * *

Emma took her overnight bag with her into the bathroom and splashed cold water on her face the minute she had shut and locked the door. She'd needed a wake-up call and, boy, had she got it.

She really didn't want to be here. The scene of all his conquests—the likes of Carolina. Jealousy raged in her. Ugly and unwanted. Unstoppable.

She took out her comb, tugging it through the twisted mess of her hair. As the car had raced along from Ellerslie she'd let the wind blow through it, whipping it into a tangle around her face, and she'd wanted it to blow away the bad feelings. Then she'd walked into his magnificent apartment and had the ground cut from under her again. He was an art lover—a serious collector, no less. And she was such an amateur. She hated being less than the best and she knew her paintings were so far from perfect. He must have been laughing the whole time.

She felt crummy, no two ways about it.

Standing under the shower, washing the travel weariness away, she tried to harden up. She knew he was a player. Had known that from the start—that there had been many before her. And, yes, it mattered. But not enough to stop her from being the next in line. She wanted him. And, if she faced facts, his knowledge of women was a plus. Surely it was the reason he could make her feel so good. Why with just a few touches he could reduce her to a heap of sensation—a woman desperate for the ultimate intimacy. She should take the experience and make the most of it. But she needed just a little longer to build up the defences around her heart again.

She slipped on her slimline satin dress, not bothering with a bra as it had such thin spaghetti straps. Besides, it wasn't as if she was going to do herself permanent damage. She tried not to think about how Carolina would fill out a little black dress. As an ego-boost she pulled on a pair of pretty panties. She looked at her reflection. If she really was a bold siren she'd go without the underwear altogether—but, while she could do that at home, in a crowded restaurant it was just one step too far out of her comfort zone.

A few touches of make-up and some shine serum on her hair

and she was done. She tipped her chin at her reflection—*deal with it.*

Back in his lounge that intention started to crumble immediately. It screamed wealthy bachelor and, as pathetic as it was, she just couldn't stop wondering how many others had been here. She gazed at the sofa. Large enough to lie on, it looked damningly comfortable.

Frustrated with her bitterness, she looked at the paintings on the walls again, only to feel even smaller. He'd seen her paintings and they were so gauche compared to these. Embarrassment washed over her. The day that had started so beautifully was turning into a nightmare.

'Where are you?'

She started.

He walked up to her, looking sexy as hell in dark trousers and linen shirt, his hair damp and slightly wayward. He stood way too close and the bad feeling began to be swallowed by desire. 'You've gone away from me. Where?'

He so didn't want to know. And she sure as hell wasn't going to tell him. Revealing her jealousy of his ex-girlfriends would reveal more than she wanted him to know. She'd gone into this with her eyes wide open—he'd told her right from the start he liked to play. And a woman like Carolina wouldn't let such a small thing as an ex-girlfriend bother her. Hell, it seemed she didn't let a thing like a current girlfriend bother her. Emma was playing with a pro and he was used to worldly types and she wasn't going to get all amateur and upset about previous competition. 'Just thinking about one of the displays today.'

He looked as if he didn't believe her, but shrugged. 'I'm glad you enjoyed it.'

'I did.' Right up to the point when Barbie appeared.

'So what do you fancy to eat—shall we go to the local steakhouse?' He was teasing her, and that tempted her. She found it hard to resist him when he was like this.

But no. She squared her shoulders and decided to up her game. She was not going to get psyched out. She was in it for the duration, could damn well learn to play hard, and maybe she'd end up a winner. 'Let's go up-market.'

His gleam of humour broke into a full grin. 'Sure.'

CHAPTER ELEVEN

THE humidity level in the evening air was high. Storm clouds threatened but when they'd walked to the club Emma hadn't been afraid of a downpour—it might've soothed her heated body. Saturday night, the start of summer and the city was alive. Not that she paid that much attention to it.

Jake had been staring at her the entire meal. She'd had to fight to stop squirming as she'd seen his attention wander over her body, to her mouth, her neck, her breast, and she'd known exactly what he was thinking, what he wanted. Exactly what she wanted. The time away from his apartment had relieved her jealousy. His undivided attention, his attraction showing so clearly, was a balm on her aggravated senses—even if that attraction was only physical and temporary. They'd said little through the meal, commented on the flower show, complimented the food, circling the real issue— the flare between them that was threatening to blow up again. Time to go home.

Then he spoke, a low voice that she still heard with clarity despite the music in the trendy club. 'Come dance with me.'

She stared back at him, with regret, not wanting to see the blaze in his eyes dim. 'I told you, I don't do dancing. I'm no good at it.'

It didn't dim, it intensified, and his lips curved as he insisted, 'We're not talking ballroom. We're talking bump and grind and I *know* you can do that.'

He took her hand and pulled her to her feet. Despite the sizzle in her fingers, her heart sank. This so wasn't going to end up like in the movies where the guy leads the girl into an applause-inducing spin on the dance floor. Where couples parted and stood back to watch in awe. More likely people would watch and laugh. The place was heaving with bodies moving in sync with the deep bass. She felt awkward. Eager to escape the sweaty couple beside her, she moved forward and trod on Jake's foot. 'See, I told you I was useless.'

He laughed, releasing a little of the pent-up energy she sensed in him. 'Come here and lean against me; I'll do the moving for both of us.' He wound his arms round her waist and drew her into length-to-length position. He nudged a foot between hers. Her lashes drooped as her senses suffered Jake overload. She couldn't say no to him, just wanted to touch and be set ablaze.

Then he moved, gently swaying her, as his strong hands guided her hips, rocking her against him, with him, to the relentless beat.

After a moment of statue-stillness as she absorbed his nearness, she gave herself over to it. Fitting in to him. The closer she got, the last lingering doubt and jealousy disappeared. Then she relaxed completely, while another tension deep inside began to tighten. The steam rose as her body softened and his became hard. A few beats later he pushed his thigh between hers and it became her support as she rode it. A temporary substitute for what she really wanted.

Breathing suddenly got really difficult. Her lips parted as she tried to get more air in. His hands weren't guiding her any more; her hips were moving of their own accord, back and forth in tandem with him. She could hardly see his face in the dark of the dance floor, but the flashing lights were reflected in his eyes as he didn't take them off her. Glittering. He lifted one hand from her back and then she felt his fingers slip beneath the hem of her dress.

This wasn't dancing. This just about wasn't legal. But it was so, so right. Thankfully the room was crowded and there were so many others on the dance floor, all intent on their own partners, or finding a partner, no one was going to be watching them.

Her hands scaled his chest and she felt the muscles tighten under her fingertips. He bent and kissed her neck as his hand slid up her thigh. He kissed her collar-bones and started to head further south while his fingers went further north. She moaned. In that instant it changed from dangerous dancing to all-out foreplay. He pulled her tighter to him as he lifted his head.

'We need to finish this in private.' His arm firm around her waist, he strode off the dance floor and she half skipped to keep pace with him.

This time as she entered his apartment she couldn't care less about who might or might not have been there before her. All that mattered was now and getting enough of him. She turned and faced him, her hands holding the hem of her dress, teasing it up as her legs parted, ready and inviting. He slammed the door behind them and tossed the keys onto the table with such force they skittered right off and onto the floor. He strode to her, stripping his shirt off at the same time. 'This is insane.'

She woke nestled in his huge bed, him half sprawled across her, his thigh heavy on her own, his arm around her, holding her close. She turned to his face and, consigning her cares to future contemplation, she woke him in the most intimate way she could.

An hour later and the sun was starting to rise high in the sky.

'I have another surprise for you.' He traced a finger down her torso.

She looked down from where she sat straddling him.

He cleared his throat. 'It means we have to get out of bed. You OK with that?'

'Do we have to?' She leant forward and smoothed her palms over his shoulders, loving the breadth, loving the freedom to touch him however she pleased.

'Yeah,' he groaned. 'It'll be fun.'

'Nothing's as fun as this.' She bent her head.

His fingers tightened around her and he lifted her away. 'Let's do this in the shower. Two birds, one stone.'

They didn't take the car, going on foot instead.

'I'm taking you to meet a friend of mine. I think you'll like her.'

Her. Emma's previously soothed hackles rose. How many of Jake's ex-girlfriends was she going to have to meet this weekend? Her blood ran even colder as he steered them into a contemporary art gallery.

'Hey, Jake.'

Emma warily watched the woman approach. She was older than she'd anticipated, dark haired with a large grey streak at the front. The epitome of urban cool, slim and wearing black, black, black. Emma thought she was not unlike Cruella de Vil. Maybe Jake had gone off-type more than once.

Then a younger woman clad in matching black, with close-cropped purple-tinged hair, came over to join her. She slipped her arm around the older woman's waist and squeezed her close. They swapped an intimate look.

Oh. Emma rebuked herself. Clearly it was possible for Jake to have female friends who weren't ex-girlfriends. Lesbian ones. She surreptitiously pinched her arm hard for being so catty.

'You must be Emma; I've been looking forward to meeting you.'

Emma blinked. Since when? She'd never heard of this woman.

'Jake emailed me pictures of some of your work. I'd be very keen to see some of them up close for myself.'

Emma froze. 'Uh.'

Jake stepped in, his hand heavy across her shoulders. 'Emma, this is Cathy. She owns the place. She's the one I told you about who keeps an eye out for me. But this time I've found something for her. I sent her photos of a few drawings and then a couple of the paintings.'

He what?

'Your drawings are superb, technically outstanding. Painstakingly detailed, but it's the paintings that really caught my attention. You use your skills, but then they're imbued with such emotion. Wonderful stuff.'

Emma was floored. She tried to turn her brain's engine on, but it appeared the battery was dead. Jake had emailed pictures? When? How?

Cruella was waffling again about the depth in her painting. Emma had never been one for art-speak. Switching off, she glanced at Jake. He was beaming at her.

'I told you they were brilliant.' He looked as if he'd done something marvellous and she wasn't able to inform him otherwise. Had he paid Cathy to go on like this? Was this whole thing a set-up?

'Are you willing to send some samples up to me?'

'I, um...' she stopped and swallowed the high-rise-sized lump in her throat '...I'd never thought much about showing them in public.'

'Well, that's why you paint, isn't it?'

Actually, no. She painted because she enjoyed it. It made her feel good. It was *hers*. And no one was judging her on it. Not until now. But a lifetime's conditioning dictated her response. Be polite. Never be rude to people you just met who are being nice to you. Don't let them down. Aim to please—others not yourself.

Cathy smiled at her silence. 'Jake told me you were shy about it, but you shouldn't be. Many artists are the same: they like to paint, but they struggle to put it out there and then stand back in the corner and hide. It takes courage, but I'm sure you're a courageous person, Emma.'

Oh. She had the whole psychology thing down pat. Emma smiled weakly. Did she have the courage to turn this woman down? Did she have the courage to tell Jake exactly what she thought of this stunt?

'Why don't you take a look around and see what you think of the kind of work I like to display?' Cathy gestured down the cleverly lit, wooden-floored space. 'We're a successful gallery.

I'm pretty good at spotting talent and we sell a lot—to clients with good taste, of course.' She laughed and winked at Jake.

Emma felt nauseous. This was so humiliating. Hot sweat covered her body and quickly turned cold. She walked away, slipping ahead of Jake so she could fix her polite mask in place. She folded her arms tight across her chest. Despite the warmth of the late-spring day, she felt as icy as a winter storm. She stopped at a large painting, blown away by its scale and execution. She could never compete with something like that—didn't want to. She wasn't a real artist, she just liked drawing flowers, for heaven's sake. She hadn't asked for this.

The soft tread of Jake's sneakers meant she didn't hear him until he was right behind her, slipping his arm around her waist just as the young woman had slipped hers around Cathy's when they'd arrived. Intimate. Knowing. But Emma was unable to swap the look of lovers.

'Fantastic, isn't it?'

Was he talking about the art or the situation? She decided to answer about the painting in front of them. 'It's beautiful.'

Melancholic, she stared around the walls. She'd been driven to succeed almost all her life and she didn't want to have to succeed here. His eyes were on her, waiting, questioning, but she couldn't give him the response he was looking for.

They slowly walked the perimeter, looking at the various works displayed.

'Will you send something?' Cathy asked as they came back to the reception area.

She tried to explain. 'I don't really do it for others. I just enjoy it.'

'Why not let others enjoy it too?' the younger woman piped up for the first time. 'It's not a competition. No one's really judging. They'll either like them or they won't. And who cares if they don't?'

Jake's arm tightened around her. 'That's what I say.'

'People would get a lift from them,' Cathy encouraged and Emma felt overwhelmed by their three-pronged attack. Railroaded into smiling and acting as if she were pleased.

The young woman spoke again. 'You'd be surprised how much we sell and how much people pay. You just have to be careful because the tax implications can be a nightmare.'

'Not a problem for Emma—she's an accountant.' Was that pride she could hear in Jake's voice? Hell, it was like her father rattling off all her accomplishments to whomever they met. Emma, the performing poodle. She glanced at him as he smiled and chatted. Did he have any idea what she felt about this? For a while there she'd thought Jake understood her. Obviously not.

Cathy handed her a card. 'Think about it. If you do decide you want to show, give me a call. I'd be interested in helping you.'

Helping? Or taking over? Setting the agenda: commissions, deadlines, orders—*pressure*. Emma didn't want to fail at this, so she refused to compete.

Walking back in the warmth of the sun, she felt frozen through to her marrow. Her art was a part of her that she'd locked away. And now Jake had come and opened it up—not just for himself, but for everyone, and she didn't like it.

She felt him look at her but she couldn't talk. She didn't know what to say, where to start. He'd gone to a lot of trouble to set up that meeting for her and part of her didn't want to knock him back for it. The pleasing part.

She stopped in her tracks as she realised what she was doing. She'd worked so hard all her childhood to please her father, now she worked damn hard to please Max.

But it wasn't supposed to be like that with Jake. Jake was for fun. Being with him was just a game—right? She was with him because it pleased *her*. The same reason she painted—for her alone. Only now he was messing with it, interfering, changing the dynamic. And she felt forced to perform—for him.

She couldn't let it happen. She couldn't let what he thought, what he wanted, matter that much. Not when this was a temporary fling. Until now he'd given her unfound freedom. By making it a game she'd been able to do whatever she wanted, say whatever she wanted and be more brazen than she'd ever dreamed. He couldn't change the rules now.

No audience. She wanted none for her passion. Except him—and he wasn't her audience, he was her playmate.

He closed the door to his apartment behind them and swung back to face her. 'You're mad with me.'

She turned to the windows, trying to keep calm. 'How did you photograph my paintings?'

She watched his reflection as he walked towards her.

'You're really mad with me.' So he did know her feelings. He did see into her—at least some of the way.

'How?'

He answered the question. 'With my phone.'

'When?' She stepped forward again, away from him. She wanted him, she'd always want him, but right now she didn't want him to touch her. She wanted to keep in control.

'The other night before we, ah…before we slept in there.'

Before she'd totally opened herself up to him. That was why he'd gone in there. *No ulterior motive?* Even if he'd thought it a good one, it still hurt her. Awfully, tears threatened. She wanted to hide.

He saw in the reflection and turned her back to face him, his hands cupping her face. 'Look, honey, I know you're scared, but your paintings are brilliant. And I'm not just saying that because I want to get in your pants. I don't know much, but I know a little about art and you have talent. You really do.'

It wasn't about talent. It was about protecting what was hers and hers alone.

'Cathy can see it too and she really does know her stuff. She wants to sell them for you.'

'I don't want to sell them.'

'At least exhibit them. You should be proud of them, you should want people to see; you should be out there promoting this.'

Should, should, should.

She didn't want him to go there—started to build the wall of reserve to cover the rawness. 'No, Jake.'

'Why not?'

'I just don't want to. Can we not talk about this any more?'

Through her anxiety she saw his frustration.

'No, we need to talk.' He sighed as she brushed his hands away and walked towards the window. 'You can't tell me you're not interested in letting people see your stuff when you're doing illustrations for a book! You can't have it both ways, Emma.'

The book was different. They were technical drawings, as exact as photographs, only more delicate. The paintings she'd done with passion and exuberance and sheer joy because they didn't matter, they didn't have to be perfect.

It finally registered that the phone was ringing and had been for some time.

'Are you going to get that?'

'No. This is more important.'

The click as the answering machine switched on stopped her from speaking.

'Jake, it's Samantha. Heard you're back in town but I can't raise you on your mobile…' Emma tried to block her voice but the words, the dulcet tones, dropped into her head like stones tossed in a shallow pool. Splashing, stirring up the mud and staying. She could just picture her—Barbie Mark II. She looked at the machine. The red indicator flashed that there were another three messages. Multiple Barbies. Bitter jealousy resurged and oozed from every pore. It tipped her balance, fuelling her anger to an irrational level.

Jake seemed not to have heard the call at all. Intently focussed on her, his argument laced with passion. 'Why hide away, Emma? Why don't you want people to appreciate your gift?' He stood next to her, talking to the side of her face. She maintained an impassive exterior and he growled, annoyance mounting. 'It's like you have this split personality. You crunch numbers by day and create amazing art at night. Everyone you work with thinks you're some workaholic icicle when you're actually this insatiable, sensual woman.'

She jerked to look at him, stunned by the even more personal direction he'd gone in. Insatiable? Sensual? Didn't he realise that was only with him?

'Why can't the world see all of you, Emma?'

'It's a hobby, that's all.'

'Bullshit. You spend hours on it. This matters to you. You told me yourself you're a perfectionist.' He swore. 'You haven't even told your parents. How can you have kept this secret from them?'

Her blood ran cold. 'I don't want them knowing, Jake.'

'Well, don't worry about me telling them.'

Given he never spoke to them, she knew there was little danger of it. 'You really don't like him, do you?'

He hesitated. 'He's your dad.'

'Yeah, but you don't like him.'

He shrugged. 'He's pushy.'

Yes. Even she could admit that—hell, the old man would admit it himself and defend it to the hilt. It made her even madder that Jake judged him like that. She knew what her father was like and she was the one who had to live with it. Not Jake. 'He is and that's the point. I don't want him or anyone else pushing expectation on me with my paintings.'

'Well, what about Margaret—aren't your drawings for her doing exactly that?'

'But that's on my terms, Jake. *My* terms. You had no right to show anyone my paintings. Why can't you understand that?'

'Your talent is too great to be shelved, Emma. Someone has to get you out from the rock you're hiding behind!'

Silence. She struggled to take in his attack. Hands on his hips, he scrutinised her. She glared back, resentment burning. For Jake everything was simple—you wanted something, you went for it. It wasn't so easy for her.

Jake was in her life temporarily but his actions—all of them—would have a permanent effect. She needed to stop him in his tracks now.

She curled her fingers into fists and fought to keep cool. Why couldn't he see that some things were for public and some for private? She didn't want to have to let him down, but he was ramping up his expectations of her. Insisting she put herself out there. Wanting her to do something she simply wasn't capable of. She locked down and called on every ounce of self-control. She breathed out slowly, quietly.

'I'm not going to change my mind, Jake. Maybe it's time you took me to the airport. I don't want to miss my flight.'

He blinked at her change in direction. 'Are you kidding?'

She turned and tried to stop him with the coldest vibe she could send his way. 'Should I get a taxi?'

It was his turn to look frosty—his face hardening, eyes shuttering.

She moved away before he answered, going to gather her belongings and toss them into her overnight bag. She glanced around his room and could scarcely believe that only a couple of hours earlier she'd lain in his bed so carelessly. Why did he have to push when for once she'd been having such fun?

He was pacing, fidgeting with the car keys in his fingers when she returned. 'Come on, Emma. Let's talk about this.'

'Leave it. There's nothing to talk about. It's my hobby, that's all. I'm not going to send them to any gallery.'

'Since when were you such a chicken? I thought you were the bravest person I know. And I can't believe I'm wrong.'

Why on earth had he thought that? She'd never been brave. She'd never stood up to her father. Never gone for what she really wanted. Only reached for her dreams in secret. Until now when she'd played out her desire for Jake in public—uncaring who knew. Not such a great move.

'I can't believe you're going to fly out of here and not sort through this with me.' He looked frustrated.

That was exactly what she was going to do. She'd opened up to him—he knew everything about her. She'd trusted him with her secrets—those of her body and her art. Thankfully she hadn't openly given him her heart.

* * *

At the airport she fiddled with the luggage label on her bag. He walked up to her, stopping too close. She looked no higher than the stripe on his casual cotton tee. He took the bag from her, peeling her fingers from the handle with a firm hand. The electricity jolted through her. Those hands could touch her ways that made her lose her mind, made her forget everything but the pleasure to be had with him. But she didn't want to let that happen now. He'd have her under his spell and she'd be saying yes—but he'd asked her something she didn't want to say yes to. She clamped down the hum of desire that ran at a constant when he was around.

'You're mad with me. OK. But let's not forget the important things, huh?' He pulled her stiff body towards him and firmly planted his lips on hers. She tasted his anger and her own and even more annoyingly it made the kiss even more divinely fiery. She felt him settle in closer, ready to drown her resistance. Only just, just, did she manage to keep under control and pull away hard. She grabbed her bag and headed through the security check before he could stop her. She heard him call her name but kept walking.

The *important* things? She'd already lost sight of them and that meant nothing but trouble.

As her plane landed she realised she didn't know when he was returning from Auckland. She rode in the taxi and couldn't stop thinking about him. Her. Her art. Her life. The way her past achievements had stifled her own aspirations. The way her upbringing had conditioned her to obey and dutifully fulfill obligations in public while keeping what mattered most a guilty secret.

The minute she was in her cottage she walked into her art room and took the key out of the door. No longer needed. She swished the curtains back. No longer secret. Jake had seen to that. She stared at the paintings. As a kid she'd dreamed of being an artist. Of living a bohemian lifestyle where she could spend her days doing her favourite thing. Of going to fine arts school. Of travelling and seeing the Masters.

She'd been told it was impossible—laughable. Her father

had done just that when as a kid she'd confessed her dream to him. He'd scoffed—did she think she was going to live some romantic, idealised life in a garret in Paris? He'd told her to wake up—you go to university and study something useful. You build a career with hard work, he'd insisted. That was how you got anywhere. That was how you earned approval—his at any rate.

Why couldn't she have been like Lucy and done it anyway? Lucy who'd kept up with her music, defiantly doing what she wanted. Refusing to follow the path their father tried to keep them on. And he still loved her, didn't he? Sure, he hassled her, but he was proud of her at the same time.

How had she got things so muddled?

Margaret's book had been like a secret gift. It had tapped into her youthful secret desire. And wasn't it enough? It was Margaret's dream—Emma was only doing some sample illustrations for her to pitch it to the publisher. She wasn't really putting her heart on the line. Showing her paintings wasn't something she'd ever felt she could do. If you were going to do something, you were going to be the best at it—that had been her mantra. And she didn't have the confidence to take the risk here.

But Jake had come along and encouraged her to do whatever, whenever—with him at least. Freeing her of anxiety by making it all a game. All the fun with him was careless—or at least meant to be. Once she was on the court with him all qualms were kept at bay by the magic of his touch. He was such a pro. She wished she could be like that for real. Wished things didn't have to matter so much.

And now, she finally admitted, *he* mattered to her—more than anything. And what he thought mattered, and what he wanted. And he wanted her to open up and he didn't realise how vulnerable she'd be if she did that.

Damn.

She stormed into the kitchen and pulled her laptop from its case. She had mountains of work to do and she had to get it done. For once she looked at it bitterly, resentment rising. She'd far rather be on the end of a paintbrush right now. But she'd told Max she wouldn't let him down. And nor would she.

Monday came and went with no word from Jake. She worked through and spent the evening on her drawings. Margaret phoned, wanting them midweek.

All her deadlines were hitting at the same time.

After nine on Tuesday night, she heard the knock on the door. His knock. She was stressed to the extreme. She had only the night to get the drawings finished and she still had work on Max's report to get through first. She pulled on the guy ropes of her helium-filled heart. She was not going to fail to complete it because of her silly crush, even if he did provide the best—and only—sex of her life. But in interfering with her decision to keep her art to herself he'd crossed the boundary and she needed to shove him back over it.

He walked straight over her threshold talking, taking the bull by the horns, excited glint in his eye. 'I've been thinking about it. So you're shy about the paintings, sure. But you could exhibit and sell them under a pseudonym—until you have the confidence to come out. Why not just send a couple and see how they do?'

He still hadn't got it and she had too much to be getting on with to go in circles. 'Jake, I told you the other day, I don't want to and I don't want to talk about it any more.'

He swept his arms around her. 'Come on, have dinner with me. Come and have me.'

Oh, she wanted him, but she wanted not to want him more. Trapped, she told herself her work was the reason. 'I can't, Jake. I have too much to do.' She pulled away, pointed at the table overloaded with papers. 'I shouldn't have gone away in the weekend.'

'Emma, you're allowed some time off.' Just like that his easy-going veneer slipped to reveal the same frustration of two days before. Neither of them had got anywhere.

'Not when it conflicts with work I have to do.'

'Why kill yourself meeting deadlines for other people? Why not show people what you really love? You haven't even shown the people you love the most!'

Hadn't she? She'd shown him—and he hadn't understood at all. He hadn't seen how important it was that painting was her private thing. And now she could only hope that that wasn't all he hadn't seen.

She desperately hoped he hadn't seen how important their affair had become to her. How jealous she'd felt when meeting Carolina, how crazily she wanted him every moment. How badly she'd fallen for him.

In love.

She had to cover up. Had to push him away, scrape a little dignity and count down every long minute until he left Christchurch again for good—to take her heart with him.

In the moment of her silence he'd hit boiling point. 'You're twenty-six years old, for God's sake. Why not just do what you want to do? Why spend your entire life trying to live up to other people's expectations? Show your paintings. You want to, Emma, I *know* you do.'

Sensory overload as his words ripped her open. This wasn't a side of Jake she could cope with. She wanted the easygoing, humorous one, not the iron-willed one prying into her deepest feelings and fears.

He must have seen her stricken expression because his manner softened. 'Come on. Come out with me. Have dinner. Relax, we can talk, eat meat if you want, drink some nice wine…'

He'd been driving her in directions she wasn't used to and suddenly it was all too much. She fought. 'Stop pushing me. Who are you to push me around like this?'

He jerked up in shock. 'Emma, I'm just concerned for you.'

'If you're that concerned for me, you'll let me get on with my work—I'm going to be up all hours to get it all done as it is.'

'What? You can't.' His volume rose with every word. 'You

can't spend an entire night on these reports, then try to finish the drawings before putting in another twelve-hour day. That's crazy.'

'I did it for enough years at uni—I know what I can do when I push hard enough,' she yelled, more than matching his decibel level. 'I'll get the drawings to Margaret, and Max needs the data and I mean to give it to him. I won't let him down.'

'He says jump, you say how high. No matter how impossible the demands, how much it impacts on your life, you do it. When are you going to learn to say no?' In her face, eyes blazing, he was wild.

'I'm saying no to you!' Not as wild as her.

The silence was sudden and deadly. They both breathed hard, but strangely she couldn't hear the air as they dragged it in.

She watched, mentally distanced as he stepped back, nodding to himself. 'So you are.'

His footsteps sounded as curt as his voice. The door slammed behind him.

She'd got her way but it was game over. Nil all.

CHAPTER TWELVE

THE hours ticked long into the night as Emma finalised the report for Max. She forced herself to focus. Once she was free and on to the drawings, she entered the 'zone' she usually loved so much when creating. But tonight was different. The scene with Jake replayed on auto. Over and over. Ugly. Pain growing with each repetition. Together with the nagging feeling that he might have been just a little bit right. That she might have been more than a bit wrong.

He'd said she was scared. OK, she admitted it—he was right about that. She was afraid—but of what? She didn't want to have to meet someone else's expectations. Because if she didn't, if she wasn't the best, she wouldn't be wanted. Let someone down and they wouldn't want you any more—wouldn't give you what you needed from them. So she hid away the things that really mattered because then they wouldn't hurt. What a stupid idea that was. Just because something was a secret, didn't mean it was safe. And wasn't life much more fun when you took the risk and shared?

She rebelled again. Damn Jake—damn him for opening her up and making her think. And feel.

She finally went to bed at six-thirty in the morning. Snatched just an hour before dragging herself from the bed and standing under the shower for even longer than usual, wanting to wash away the tiredness and the ache. It didn't work.

* * *

She went into the art room and studied the last of the drawings she'd completed through the night. Not bad. She knew they were good to go. She'd given it her all. She carefully slipped the illustrations into the portfolio together with the clean copy of Margaret's manuscript. She looked at the table, looked at her work on the walls, and with a spark of defiance she lifted a couple of canvases. She wrapped them carefully and put them into the carry case. Phoned the courier company before she changed her mind. They were gone by eight-fifteen and there was no going back.

So there Jake Rendel.

She practically ran to work. She had already emailed the final report through to Max well past midnight, but she wanted to be there to address any questions he might have. She knew he would have been in at work since half seven and would have read it by now.

Her phone rang almost the moment she sat down. Her heart stopped. She answered, breathless, and grimaced at her weakness.

'Emma, it's Margaret. Just got your package. They're perfect, absolutely perfect. I knew you were the one to ask. I'm so confident they'll go for us. Thank you so much.'

It took a moment to switch gears. She'd so hoped it would be Jake. 'Well, we've tried, haven't we?'

'We sure have. The paintings you've included are just fabulous.'

'Oh.' She already regretted that. 'You can leave them out if you want to. They were just something I was having fun with.'

'Leave them out? No way! They're the icing, they really are.'

Emma didn't know whether she wanted to laugh, cry or vomit. What was she doing? Her nerve hardened. She was playing by *her* rules.

Next call was Max. She forced the air from her lungs. He was happy with the report and scheduled a full staff meeting for late afternoon. She slumped in her chair, running on nothing, and couldn't even face the idea of chocolate. She'd done it. Margaret had the drawings and was happy. Max had his report and was happy. She'd achieved what she'd set out to do—but so what? Was she happy? Crowd-pleasing wasn't all it was cracked up to be when you started to wonder about what ends you were working to. Not her own. She'd always been reliable, capable Emma—efficient and above reproach. Since when had that translated into so thorough, so diligent—so doormat?

Jake tried to stroll casually into the hotel but knew the way his fists were clenched around his jacket and briefcase that it was a dead loss. Muffled thumping from upstairs indicated the boys had begun part of the demolition work for the day. He was waylaid by Becca for a few minutes' meaningless chitchat. As he struggled to extricate himself from her his attention was suddenly arrested by the sight of Emma in conversation with the doorman. He watched as the guy leant forward on his desk, body language all a go-go. Jake tensed. He knew the jealousy was totally a double standard. But he couldn't bear the thought of her getting close up with anyone but him. Ironic when he'd hardly been lily-white. Girls aplenty in his past. But not now. He'd lost his appetite for anyone but her.

She looked relaxed, and certainly didn't look as if she'd been up all hours working her butt off. She sure as hell didn't look as if she'd spent a moment's worry about how things had ended with him last night. He had no idea whether she cared or not and it was eating him up. He wanted her to care. Wanted it all to matter the way it did to him. The pleasure he got from her pleasure was scary. He loved to see her loose and laughing. *Loved.*

Now *that* was scary. His instinct was to fight it—fear confused with anger.

He finally got away from Becca and walked over. He interrupted the conversation and saw the veil pull across her eyes, the smile fade. He glared at the door guy who backed off immediately. Good. 'Did you get it all done?'

She nodded.

Foolishly he couldn't help setting himself up again. 'Are you going to have dinner with me tonight?'

She looked away. 'No, I...'

That word again. The one he hated to hear fall from her—especially so quickly and so casually. She didn't care. He consciously relaxed the muscles in his jaw. So it was game over. He felt like picking up one of the sledgehammers upstairs and knocking down that partition wall himself—blow by blow.

She elaborated—eventually. 'I have to meet with a couple of catering companies for Mum. Their party is coming up.'

He knew the one. 'Second Saturday in December. The highlight of my social calendar.' She frowned at his sarcastic drawl. The Delaney 'Start of summer/Wedding anniversary/Christmas' bash—renowned in the town. Old Lucas had his lawns manicured for it, usually put a marquee out the back, hired a band and invited the world. Everyone came and Lucas stood forth and showed off his beautiful house, beautiful wife and beautiful daughters. Jake bristled.

His mum always went, Sienna too. But he'd never bothered despite his name being on an invite every year. *Jake & Partner*. It had been bad enough seeing it all from his room above the garage as a youth. Lucas and his overt display of wealth and success and his hard-pushed daughters. If only he knew the half of it.

Jake's blood boiled over. 'How can you go home and be the dutiful daughter when they don't know half of what's going on in your life? The things that are most important to you?'

The veil lifted to reveal the fire in her eyes. Flames of anger, but he couldn't help but think he saw desire too. 'Everybody has secrets, Jake.'

'Not like this.'

'I take it you won't be going.' She gave a scornful laugh.

With savage satisfaction he was able to give her answer back to her. 'No. I sure won't.'

'Of course not. Wouldn't want to see my father and me having a good time. It would ruin your perception of him being the ogre and all.'

'Perception? You're the one who's keeping your life a secret. What are you so scared of if it's not him?'

The fire in her eyes flared, that whisker of desire obliterated. 'Maybe it's interference, Jake. Maybe I don't want him or anyone else meddling in something that is my business.'

'You think I was meddling? I was trying to help you...'

Her eyes widened further and, stunned, he saw the anger in her ignite. 'I don't need your help, Jake. I don't want your pity. You don't have to feel sorry for me. So don't throw your weight around where it's not wanted. Just back off!'

His jaw dropped. He'd never, ever seen Emma as wound up as this and it wasn't just anger he saw, but fear and a hurt, hunted look. Before he could process it his brain ticked over into defence mode. How had this gone so wrong? Did she really think he was that overbearing? It hadn't been that bad, for goodness' sake. She was acting as if he'd committed the crime of the century.

She turned and he watched, too angry to move, as she went to the lift and pressed the button to summon it. She stood with her back to him, no glance back. Interference? He'd been trying to help her—and she needed it. She was hiding away and living some half-life when she should be celebrating and making the most of her talents—all of them. But if she wasn't able to see it, or want it, then fine. He didn't need the grief. He'd head back to Auckland and have some fun. This was just too much like hard work. The breath steamed out of him.

Relax.

Yet kid as he might and tell himself to 'chill', he couldn't because it hurt. The deadlock made his bones ache. Trying to release the clamp in his jaw was mission impossible now. He could smash that partition with his bare hands. He spun on his heel. As he strode past Reception Becca called to him. 'She did it, huh?'

He looked at her, wondering what she was on about.

'Emma.' Becca jerked her head towards the lift into which Emma had disappeared. 'Broke your heart.'

It was a little too close to the bone and every muscle screamed tighter with tension.

'I'm good at repair jobs.' She delivered the blatant invitation with a vivacious smile.

For once he couldn't laugh it off and, ignoring the fact he was supposed to be going to a meeting with his foreman, ignoring the woman leaning towards him suggestively, he walked straight out of the hotel wanting as far away from this mess as possible.

The day dripped by. Emma's blood boiled with bitterness. What had happened to the laid-back game they'd been playing? She'd been such a fool—got too involved, taken it too seriously. And he hadn't taken her seriously enough.

He'd been trying to help her. *Because he felt sorry for her.* So humiliating. Here she was in love with the guy and he was still just being 'nice' to the overly conscientious geek girl. Showing her a little fun—something to while away the time he was down here. She'd seen him talk to Becca when he came in. All smiles for the blonde beauty. Her strung-out nerves had snapped at that. It would be no time until another woman caught his interest. Well, she wasn't going to hang around waiting to get tossed aside. She'd ended it—saving herself from further hurt and humiliation.

The bitterness grew. She didn't know if it was possible to feel more hurt. She worked up her anger to cover it. His antagonism towards her father and the party was a good place to start. Truth be told, she didn't much enjoy the event either, but she'd always, always show up for her parents—as would Lucy. She might not want to share everything with them at this stage in her life, but that didn't mean she didn't love them. Loyalty was a big thing. He was loyal to his mother and Sienna; of course she was loyal to her parents. Even if her dad was pushy, deep down she knew he only wanted the best for her.

She dragged herself to the staff meeting in Max's office and read through the financial summary for them. Braced herself while Max discussed the progress of the refurbishments. They'd just finished discussing this when Becca spoke. 'Wasn't Jake going to give us an update?'

All heads swivelled in Emma's direction. One of those please-let-the-ground-eat-me-up moments. She tried to look dignified and hoped her blush was more of a four than a ten on her usual scale. She looked to Max for the answer. He too was looking at her, thoughtfully, and she read concern in his expression. He eventually filled the silence.

'I believe he got called back to Auckland on business.'

She knew Becca was still looking at her. She could see the small smile and thought ugly thoughts for a second. Then she thought about what she was going to do. He'd gone, relieved her of the necessity, but she still wanted to escape.

She waited until the others had left Max's office. He looked at her but quickly glanced away, seeming to know she needed a rest from relentless scrutiny. 'What's up, Emma?'

'I'm sorry for the short notice, but do you mind if I take a few days off?'

He tapped something on his computer before asking blandly, 'How long do you need?'

'Just until the end of the week. I'll be back Monday.'

He typed some more. 'So long as you leave everything tied up and detailed notes, then I see no problem.'

She'd just reached the door when he called her name. She stopped and turned back to him.

He smiled at her. 'Have a good break.'

She squared her shoulders, trying to hide the horrendous confusion inside. 'I will. Thanks, Max.'

She stayed late, working to tie up the loose ends and make notes should anything arise in the next week that needed answering. All the while she kept her mind a blank. Focusing on one task and then the next, calmly, methodically, until at last her desk was clear and computer shut down. She was ready to leave.

Only then did she glance at her specimen vase. The tulip and the little forget-me-not were well past their best. Petals withered and about to drop. Beautiful while they lasted, but ultimately doomed to fade. She picked up the vase and tipped the entire contents into her waste-paper basket. Looping the strap of her bag over her arm, she walked out and didn't look back.

knowing he'd missed all the way and upend the entire thing onto her again and—hell, I forgive the error of her fears but now she whatshisname and then I knew better.

CHAPTER THIRTEEN

JAKE frowned at the small-scale building model and pretended he was listening to the architect next to him, all the while mentally beating himself up. It was his own silly fault. He'd set himself up completely. Offered to be Emma's plaything. Only now she didn't want to play. And nor did he. He wanted the real deal and she wanted it over.

He'd always been a champion player and that was how she saw him. But now he wanted different. The realisation was slow and painful and he fought it. He hated the way his feelings for her and the situation he was in were so beyond his control.

He vacillated. It wouldn't work. Couldn't. He didn't do serious. Didn't do commitment. And he definitely didn't do distance. She had a huge job in Christchurch that she loved and put above everything else. And he couldn't move either. People counted on him. He had to forget the idea of her in his future and just keep the memory of a fun few weeks. Now he could move on to something new and exciting.

So why did it feel as if his heart had been skinned?

He gave the architect a set smile and escaped to his car.

He still wanted her and could have sworn he'd still seen desire in her face when they'd parted. If she'd felt that, then he still had a chance. She was just mad with him for forcing her hand.

He hunted for common ground—literally. He didn't have a

patch of earth in his penthouse apartment. He frowned. But he did have the roof. He could have a pot garden on the roof. And there were lots of hotels in Auckland—they'd need accountants. His pulse quickened.

Maybe he had stuffed up. Pushed too far. But he'd wanted to help. If he confided in Sienna she'd roast him properly. She was always on at him for interfering in her life. And yet, he couldn't regret it. Maybe he'd gone about it wrong, maybe he should have talked it through with Emma first, but he'd thought going to the gallery and meeting Cathy like that, hearing her evaluation direct, might get through to her better than he could.

It frustrated him beyond belief that this vibrant, warm woman struggled to express her desires. But with him she had. And that was why he'd done it, because he was sure that deep down she wanted to paint, and for people to know it. She was just stuck where she was because she thought it was where she had to be. He hated that she was too busy meeting other people's expectations to be making the most of her talents and maximising her pleasure in life. Many people didn't have that, weren't able to combine career with something they loved, but Emma could if she wanted, and he'd wanted to show her that. When he set his mind to something he could usually succeed and he liked to be able to put that to use for those he loved.

And there was the rub.

It wasn't just some fun affair. A game that went a little further than they'd intended. He hadn't been having sex with her.

He'd been making love.

For the first time.

And, stupidly, he'd only just realised it.

Was it too late? He gripped the steering wheel. It couldn't be. He was in love. A damn awful situation to be in and one he'd never imagined. The ironic laugh jerked out. All this time he'd been off kilter with wanting her. Needing her so bad he could hardly think straight—because at the back of his mind was the knowledge that she wasn't going to be his for long. He'd always said he didn't want to settle—he just wanted to have fun.

Life with Emma was fun.

Life without her wasn't.

The solution hit him like the thunderbolt from the heavens. The only way to cure the discomfort Emma brought him was to ensure Emma was with him for good.

He took in a deep breath. Felt better for the realisation. Then panicked.

How was he to convince *her*? She had no basis for comparison. How did he get her to understand that what they shared wasn't normal—that there would never be better than this? As far as she was concerned they were just playing around with him in the role of her 'get-some-experience' guy. She didn't want or expect serious from him. She'd just shoved his serious intention to help her straight back in his face.

He toyed with his phone, but knew it wasn't the answer. Too complicated—he needed face to face. He cursed his hotheaded decision to blow out of Christchurch and get back to Auckland. But he'd been mad with her overreaction. Hurt that she could switch off from him so easily. Scared that her coldness meant she didn't care.

So if he was to convince her, he had to speak to her in a language she'd understand.

Emma's mobile buzzed. She pulled the car over and flipped the phone open, trying not to be disappointed when it wasn't Jake on the caller display. She so had to get over him. Good thing she'd ended it when she had. It was enough of a killer as it was—her heart punctured by a thousand shards of glass.

She pressed the answer button. Margaret's excited voice burst into the silence of the car. The publisher wanted it. All of it: her drawings, Margaret's text—*the paintings*.

'By rights you should get first billing because without your drawings there wouldn't be a book. Look, I shouldn't be telling you this because the publisher is going to call you direct, but they're already talking about spin-off items. They want to do some stationery and maybe even a calendar featuring your work.

He's already asking me if I knew if you had other stuff. Have you got other paintings?'

Emma paused, life at a crossroads.

Should she stay on the straight, flat road or go for the no-speed-limit motorway that led who knew where? A crash on that one could be fatal. But the other option would be fatally boring. Jake's cheeky grin appeared in her mind's eye, daring her to be bold, to say what she truly wanted—to herself and the rest of the world.

She closed her eyes, holding on to the image. 'I've got loads more.'

Twenty minutes later she sat in the café on the coast, the seagulls circling the car park, the decaf latte perfect. She clutched the cup with her shaking hands. Breathing deep, she looked around the décor. Paintings done by a local artist adorned the walls. Signs beneath each one giving title, medium and price. Simple. Little ad hoc sales generating a small, haphazard income. And then a plan began to form. One way of having it all—career-wise at least. She might have lost Jake but he'd never been hers to keep anyway, and maybe she could take something from the experience, what he'd taught her. She could apply the freedom to have fun and still achieve. To relax, be herself and do what she wanted—her own way.

First thing Monday morning after those few days tripping round the coastline, sketching ideas and images, Emma gathered her nerves and wobbly emotions. Clicking on the print icon, she picked up the paper on the way out and walked straight to Max's office before she lost her nerve.

His door was open and she rapped on it lightly to get his attention. He looked up from the documents in front of him and his gaze went unerringly to the sheet she held.

He spoke before she had a chance. 'I've been expecting this.'

His prescience was scary. She looked at him in surprise.

'Is it to travel or is it for love?'

She sank into the chair across from him, knees giving way in the relief that he already knew, and that he didn't appear too hurt or cross. She put the letter of resignation on his desk. 'Actually, it's a slight change in direction career-wise.'

He tapped his forehead with his finger. 'Should have known it wouldn't be the obvious.' He smiled, reassuring. 'I knew I wasn't going to have you for ever, Emma. And nor should I. You should be off chasing dreams.' He leaned back in his chair with a satisfied sigh. 'I'm off to chase mine shortly. On the golf course. Retirement!'

She knew then the phrase 'nobody is indispensable' deserved to be a cliché. He wasn't; she wasn't. The hotel wasn't going to fall over in a heap because the two of them were departing. Fresh changes would probably bring fresh vitality. She warmed. 'You've worked hard.'

'So have you, and in the last few years we've done a wonderful job together.' He stood and headed to his mini bar. 'Drink?'

'At this time of the day?' It was barely after nine.

'Mmm. Right as ever, Emma. Let's go for ice cream instead.' Max had an insatiable love of frozen ices. They walked out of his office and out of the hotel towards the natural ice-cream shop he haunted. 'The company will be disappointed. They know what an asset you are.'

She flushed and shook her head. 'I just crunch numbers. Anyone with the training can do that.'

He shook his head. 'You have a work ethic second to none.'

The waitress had seen them approach and had his wild berry frozen yoghurt ready on the counter. Emma ordered triple chocolate and ignored Max's appalled noises. 'I'm sorry I can't last the distance for you, Max.'

'Don't be silly. I'm lucky to have held on to you as long as I did. Thanks to you I'm leaving on a high—the hotel is in excellent shape, will be wonderful once the extensions are done. It sold for a mint. I couldn't be happier. And now you're off to pastures new. It's exciting for both of us.' He took a giant bite of his cone with his front teeth.

Valiantly ignoring the goose-bumps Emma got on his behalf, she grinned. 'Thanks, Max.'

He winked. 'And what about that man?'

'Which man?' The chill she felt was harder to ignore this time.

'Jake, you know, the one who made you smile.'

She licked her ice cream to delay answering while she tried to think of something noncommittal.

Max got in first. 'He seemed very taken with you.'

Hell, he was getting soppy in his old age.

'I thought you were going to have some fun as well as work hard?'

Emma cleared her throat.

Max sighed. 'Shame, I thought you were well suited. Still, plenty more fish in the sea.'

Just not any Emma wanted to catch.

He left her at Reception as Becca gestured her over.

'Some flowers arrived for you while you were away. We tried calling you at home but there was no answer so we put them in the staff room. They're gone now—the cleaner must have taken them away in the weekend.'

'Was there a note?'

She shook her head.

Emma nodded. Not wanting to meet Becca's piercing gaze, she turned to go back up to her office, but stopped as she thought of something. 'Do you know what kind of flowers they were?'

Becca frowned. 'No, it was all the one type, but I don't know what they were.' She paused. 'Not roses.'

'What colour?'

'White.'

Not tulips either; everyone recognised those.

She went back to her office, determined to forget about it.

Now she'd made her decision she'd hoped the days would slide by faster, but each hour seemed to go slower and slower still. She grappled with the simplest of tasks—heart not in it—and counted away the minutes.

Jake stared at the block in front of him and contemplated the night ahead. He couldn't remember the last time he'd been home alone night after night like this, but he really didn't feel up to going out.

A bit of time and perspective usually did wonders, but it wasn't helping in this case. He could kick himself. He should have listened, should have seen the extent of her anxiety. Now he worried he'd broken her trust by showing Cathy her work when she wasn't ready. But he was a man of action. Too much, too soon—the story of their whole affair.

He'd needed some time to get to grips with what was happening and clearly she still needed more. He refused to believe he could feel this strongly and she not. He ached all over. He had to make this right. It had been days and he'd heard nothing. He glanced at his mobile. Silent, still and he was not going to pick it up and press buttons. If she hadn't understood the flowers, he'd find another way. Never a quitter, he always had a backup plan. Trouble was he might need more than one in this case and he didn't know if his heart could handle the suspense. He picked up his chisel. One scrape at a time.

When Emma got home that night she found a beat-up blue car parked outside her cottage. Oh, great. Talk about lowering the value of the neighbourhood.

'Well, if it isn't Tweedledum and Tweedledummer.' Lucy and Sienna sat parked on her veranda, bottle of wine already open. She summoned a grin for them and trudged up the two stairs.

'Hello, Ms Workaholic. We've been here for *hours*.' Lucy raised her glass at her.

Emma looked at the almost-empty wine bottle and the grease-stained fish and chip wrappers. 'No kidding.'

She sat down on the top step, took Lucy's glass from her hand and drained it.

Lucy stared open-mouthed. 'Bad day?'

One of many this last week. Despite handing in her resignation and starting work on a new painting, she couldn't shake the blues. Couldn't stop thinking about Jake. It frustrated her beyond belief. She'd always been a career girl and now she stood on the brink of a new and exciting venture and all she could think about was some bloke.

But he wasn't just any bloke and that was the problem.

She couldn't bear to look Sienna in the eyes. They were the exact same blue as Jake's. Only Sienna had a mass of hair the colour of strawberry-tinted gold, not the thick, black, slightly unruly cut that Jake had.

'We're only here for the one night, sister. OK if we crash?' Lucy poured the remainder of the bottle into her glass and handed it to Emma.

'Sure, where are you headed?'

'Going walking—Milford Track.'

Emma nearly choked on the last of the wine. 'Since when were you two so energetic?' These two were total urbanites. She couldn't help a sideways glance at Sienna. Milford Track was one of New Zealand's most glorious walking tracks—but quite a hike. Because of her heart condition Sienna had been banned from strenuous physical activity almost all her life, until she'd taken up the drums in utter defiance of the medical profession— and her mother. And Jake.

Sienna caught the look and answered the implied question. 'I'm crossing off a few items on my life's "to do" list.'

'Yeah, and I'm on the prowl for gorgeous Scandinavian tourists.' Lucy leered.

'The ones backpacking with their gorgeous Scandinavian girl-friends,' Emma flattened her drily.

'Bah humbug.'

Emma stood and stretched. 'Come on inside. You've had dinner whereas I'm starving.' She wasn't really, but it gave her something to do. She rummaged in the fridge for a pack of smoked salmon and ferreted some crackers from the cupboard.

The two sat at the table and regaled her with tales of club life in the capital, Wellington. It made Emma's head ache and so she halted it with ease—by nagging them about their futures. 'So, what do you do with a music degree, girls?'

Lucy screwed up her face. 'Ugh, don't. You sound like Dad.'

'Or Jake,' Sienna added.

At the mention of his name Emma's hands wobbled. Her heart did more than wobble. It lurched. But she decided to be bold and mention him. Sienna must know they'd seen each other down here. She just hoped she didn't know how much of each other they'd seen. 'I saw him at the hotel a bit but I think he's gone back to Auckland now. Did you want to catch up with him?'

'Hell, no, the last thing I need is him sticking his oar in. He'll be wanting to arrange my career for me—fixing up an interview or something.' She gave a mock shiver.

Emma stared at her.

Sienna laughed at her expression. 'Seriously, you think your dad is bad, he's nothing on Jake.' She sat back in her chair and launched forth. 'Jake fixes things—it's what he does. Buys buildings and fixes them. Arranges deals. Makes oodles of money and keeps foisting it on to us. He's forever going on to Mum to retire when it's the last thing she wants to do. He hasn't learnt he can't do it all for us all the time.' Her fingers beat a steady tattoo on the table. 'Can you imagine his frustration when he couldn't fix *me*?'

Lucy handed her a glass of water but it didn't stop the tirade.

'And now he doesn't seem to realise I'm perfectly capable of achieving something on my own. He still won't let me carry my own bag—if he saw that camping pack he'd have a fit. He thinks he's helping. I know he just wants the best for me, wants it to be easy for me. But he doesn't understand that I want to do it myself—'

'Don't grump, Sienna,' Lucy chided. 'It's how he shows he cares.'

Emma frowned at her salmon and looked up to see Sienna looking at her with an apologetic expression. 'Don't get me wrong. I love the guy to bits and I'll always be grateful for what he's done for me. But I'm grown-up and healthy and he doesn't have to worry any more. I can take care of myself.' She reached for a cracker, but it didn't make it to her mouth; instead it became a quasi-drumstick with a life of its own, beating on the table. 'He's been so busy concerning himself with me and Mum, he's burnt out.'

'Burnt out?' Emma couldn't see that. Jake had more energy than anyone she'd ever met.

'In the sense he won't have a long-term relationship. Goes through girls like you wouldn't believe.' The cracker snapped. 'Two months tops, then he trades them in. And the thing is some of them are actually quite nice.' She shrugged. 'But he says he just wants to have fun. He's always felt responsible for us and doesn't want more responsibility with a serious girlfriend. Then again, maybe he just hasn't met the right one yet.'

For the kazillionth time in her life Emma wished her skin weren't so pale that even the tiniest hint of a blush showed like a stop sign. The right one? How she wished that had been her. But she'd just been the geek one. The one he'd felt sorry for. His interest had come on the back of that. She attributed it to novelty factor— a game going a few steps too far. He enjoyed women, and she was no more special than any of them. She hadn't even gone the usual distance. Two months? She'd had less than two weeks. A huge chunk of her, the naughty, recently discovered live-on-the-edge and take-what-you-want side wanted the six or so weeks she was missing.

Badly.

The rational, protective, sensible part told her she'd had a lucky escape because any longer in his bed and she'd be a complete wreck when he ended it and found someone else.

She suddenly realised Sienna had stopped talking and that she'd been abnormally silent. Lucy gave her a long look but said nothing.

Emma stood and got a couple of bars of Caramello from the freezer. Distraction always worked with wayward sisters and their friends.

'Mind if I look around your cottage? It's so cute.'

Sienna was on her feet and walking down the hall before either Lucy or Emma could speak.

The shriek was instant as she went into the art room. 'Emma, this is amazing! I never knew.'

Lucy shot Emma a look and mouthed 'sorry'.

Emma shrugged. It was OK. It was going to have to be OK because she was going public—in print, no less.

She stepped into the room after Sienna and stared at the half-tubes of paint smeared on her palette—wasted. She'd spent over two hours trying to mix the exact shade of green she was after and had failed. In everything this week, she was off her stroke.

Morosely she contemplated the upcoming weekend. 'You're coming to the parents' party, aren't you?'

'Absolutely.' Sienna's distracted answer came as she studied the painting of the wisteria.

'Wouldn't dream of missing it,' Lucy added bluntly, winking at Emma. 'I hear you've been sorting out some of the catering.'

'You know how it is. Mum wants something splendid. Something from the city that you can't get at home.'

'I had no idea you painted.' Sienna was working her way around the walls. 'These are fantastic. You know, Jake collects art—you should show him.'

Emma stared at the abandoned picture of the gardenia and swallowed the irony.

She set the two of them up in the lounge. They unrolled their sleeping bags happily and said they were in training for the hiking trip. Emma winced. The idea of camping was romantic, but the reality of bugs, hard ground, sand and damp irritated her. Give her a hotel any day. She lay in her bed listening to the muffled sounds as they settled down for the night. It wasn't long before quiet descended over the cottage. She looked through the chink in her curtain at the streetlight.

It's how he shows he cares.

Deep inside that greatest of human traits flickered—hope.

She tried to squash it. Of course he cares—as he cares for his sister. She was the quiet, studious neighbour he'd *felt sorry for.* But images of them being utterly adult flashed through her mind.

Had he really been feeling sorry for her then? He wasn't doing *that* to make her feel better.

He'd wanted her. Again and again.

She tried once more to kill the hope—he wanted anything in a skirt. A player enjoying the novelty of a skinny brunette. Heat ran through her as the devilish side asserted dominance—so what? You were enjoying him too. Wasn't it possible just to go back to the game? Ignore the reality of the impact, the consequences of the end result?

Her heart pounded as she dared herself. She just had to get through the party at the weekend and then maybe she'd go and demand the remainder of her two months. Could she do it without more damage to her heart?

What had Jake said: if you don't ask, you don't get?

She'd grown the courage to go for what she really wanted career-wise; could she take the same risk with her passion for Jake? Fight the fear and ask for what she wanted: him—for however long it lasted.

CHAPTER FOURTEEN

JAKE headed UP the stairs with a heavy tread and a heavy heart. This was his last shot. And he was terrified.

Emma's father stood on his deck, lord of the manor, watching him arrive.

'Jake.'

'Lucas.'

'Nice to see you here. You coming to the party later?'

'Maybe.'

'How can I help?'

'Actually I was looking for Emma.'

Lucas stared at him. 'She's not here.'

It was as if a ten-tonne safe had landed on his chest.

'She's gone to get some flowers for the party tonight.'

Jake exhaled, the crush on his ribs easing. The disappointment in that fraction of an instant had nearly caused a cardiac arrest.

Lucas's gaze sharpened and then he looked away. 'You see her in Christchurch?'

'A bit.' Every delectable inch of her.

'She seem happy?'

Jake was stunned into silence. He looked at the older man and for the first time noticed lines—of age and worry.

Lucas gazed into middle distance. 'She doesn't seem too happy.'

Jake's heart-rate picked up. Had she confided in her father? Was he about to get a 'you be good to my daughter' lecture? He half hoped so. Hoped she was as miserable as him because things had gone wrong.

But, no, she'd never have told her father a thing about their affair. Not when she hadn't told him about her art, about a whole other degree she'd achieved.

Lucas sighed. 'All you want for your kids is the best. Want them to do OK, be OK. You try to teach them what's important. And all you seem to do is stuff up.'

Jake cleared his throat; he didn't quite know what to say. Nothing was needed, apparently; Lucas continued without prodding. 'Neither Emma nor Lucy seem as happy as I'd want.'

Hardly surprising. Lucy had spent the latter half of her teens so far off the rails that only now was she straightening out—largely thanks to Sienna. Jake had no idea to what extent Lucas knew of what Lucy had been up to in that time. Probably little. It seemed his daughters weren't exactly open with him.

'You did good, Jake. You work hard, like Emma. You've got money to burn.' He looked him in the eye. 'You happy?'

Jake looked over the gardens and took a deep breath as he thought about his reply. 'There are a couple of things I need to sort.'

Lucas nodded. 'Sienna?'

Jake frowned. Nope, for once in his life he hadn't been thinking about her at all.

'I know how much you've done for her and your mother. Such a worry all those years. But she's OK now, isn't she?'

Jake nodded slowly. Sure, she had a fixed-up heart and the doctors saw no reason to think she couldn't live a full normal life.

The older man laughed roughly. 'I once said you'd come to nothing if you left school at sixteen. Remember?'

He could hardly forget.

'Wrong, wasn't I? Mind you—' he frowned '—I've been wrong about a few things.'

They both stood and contemplated the garden.

'You were just trying to help me, Lucas. You thought you were doing me a favour, but I had to do it my way.' He frowned. He'd been doing to Emma exactly what her old man had tried to do to him. Thinking his way was it, bullying her into showing her paintings when she'd needed to do things her way, in her own time. Knucklehead. But he was a man so used to being in control and he could control nothing when it came to Emma. Certainly not his feelings. And as a result he'd come down too heavy.

'Emma's OK,' Jake said finally. She would be; come hell or high water he'd do something, anything, to make it work.

Lucas turned to him. 'Can I get you a beer?'

Emma cursed as she lifted the bunch of Christmas lilies into the car. Typical, she'd got yellow pollen from the stamens all over her white tee shirt and down her dark denim skirt. Permanent stains. The story of her life at the moment. Permanent mark on her heart too. Lucy looked at her. 'Are you sure you're OK?'

'Yeah, I'm sure.'

Lucy sighed. 'That's just so not true, but if you're not ready to talk, fine. I know something's up.' She sniffed. 'Can you lighten up a bit, though? The damn party's hard enough to live through if I don't have you on board.'

They got in and Lucy pulled away from the kerb. 'Is it a bloke?'

Emma said nothing.

'I've never seen you like this so I'm figuring it *must* be a bloke.'

A whisker of amusement slipped from Emma. 'I'll be OK, Luce.'

'I know. You always are.' Lucy checked the rear vision. 'Be good to be more than OK for once, though, wouldn't it?'

Emma struggled to get out of the car without crushing the flowers and making even more of a mess of her top.

Slamming the door shut with her foot, she turned to walk up the path laden with the fragrant blooms.

'Hey, Jake, long time!' Lucy sang out.

Emma jerked her head up to see her father sitting on the top step of the deck, beer in hand. And next to him, beer also in hand, sat Jake. A bowl of cashew nuts sat between them. The party seemed to have started early. And it was more of a shock than if they'd lined up a bunch of geriatric strippers.

Compelled by forces way beyond her control, she looked at Jake, meeting his gaze, and she stood still on the path while he looked her over. Even from the distance between them she could see the glimmer of amusement in his eyes, the gleam of desire. Then it faded and they sombrely stared at each other.

She was glad she was holding the massive bunch of flowers because it gave her something to cling to instead of running and clinging to him. She'd give herself away completely, willing to take anything he offered, just wanting him again and having him for as long as he could offer. It was humiliating. She wanted it, but she wanted it on her own terms and she needed some time to compose herself.

He carefully set his glass down beside him and pulled to his feet.

Then Emma became aware that both her father and sister were staring at the two of them, heads swivelling back and forth like the open-mouthed clowns in the sideshow-stall attraction. And she had the horrible feeling her heart had been written all over her face.

Jake spoke. 'I wanted to have a word, Emma.'

Nobody moved for an instant as the four of them exchanged looks.

Lucy suddenly swung into action. 'Dad, you take the lilies from Emma.'

Her brain not functioning, Emma argued. 'I have to do the display.'

Lucy passed stems to her father, who had walked down to meet them. 'You're not the only one who knows how to put flowers in a vase.'

Jake walked down the stairs and along the path to where she

still stood. Lucy carried the flowers past him and inside, flashing him a warm smile. Her father was looking sideways at them and weaving up the path as a result.

Her attention snapped back to Jake. 'What are you doing here?' Work, it had to be work.

'Waiting for you.'

She ordered her heart-rate to slow down; she could hardly think with its beat thumping so loud and fast in her ear. 'But this is the one event on your social calendar you always miss.'

He closed his eyes, blocking her view to his frustration and whatever other emotions he was feeling. When he opened them again the turmoil was blanked. 'Emma. I wanted to see you. I have something for you.'

The fog of shock and confusion cleared and she was able to see him, really see him and take in his appearance. She'd always love him in jeans and a tee. But today he looked a little thinner, needed a shave and he looked tired.

'You've been working long hours.' She realised she'd spoken aloud.

'No worse than you, I imagine.'

If only he knew. And soon enough he would. She planned to tell him everything. Just as soon as she got the guts.

They stared at each other as silence fell again, awkward, unbreakable. She felt the flush mount in her cheeks. Was he remembering the same things she was? The way he felt, the things they'd done? Did he want it all over again as she did right now?

Incredibly she saw an answering rise of colour slash his cheeks. 'I, er, I have it in my garage.'

'Oh.' She pulled her shoulders back and down, willing the wobble in her legs to vamoose. Could he see the shakes she had? The physical impact of his presence knocked her sideways—literally.

She straightened up and put one foot in front of the other, letting him go slightly ahead so he couldn't see her look such an idiot. The garage stood on the boundary between her parents' property and his mother's. Two storeys—a flight of stairs ran up the outside to get to the workshop upstairs, where his grandfather had spent most of his time whittling wood, and where Jake had spent many hours keeping him company. His mother's car hadn't been parked in the garage in decades—it was too full storing bikes and benches and Sienna's old drum kits. She used to practise there—Jake had lined the walls with soundproofing board and Sienna and Lucy had spent hours in there, practising, gossiping and being girls.

With the woodworkers upstairs and the musicians downstairs it was a little shack of hobbyists. And one party that Emma had never been in on.

Jake led her in, heading straight to one of the benches lining the far wall. The gloomier light meant her eyes took a moment to adjust.

'I made you something for Christmas.' For the first time she could recall, Jake sounded vaguely uncertain.

She looked to the bench that held his complete attention. On top of it stood a boxy shape covered in soft cloth.

'It's a little early and not exactly wrapped—sorry.'

He stood aside, waiting for her to step forward, still not looking her in the eye. She reached out and lifted off the cloth.

A wooden box, about the size of a microwave, highly polished. She recognised the wood as rimu—reddish, native to New Zealand. Carved around the edges and sides was a border— a simple daisy chain. The same chain was carved on the top of the lid, but this time as a frame for a carved picture in the centre of the lid. She blinked. Instinctively she lifted her hand and traced her finger in the groove he'd chiselled out with such skill.

She felt the blood drain and her vision blurred as a faint threatened. She knew the picture. It was the one she'd drawn in her office that day—of the tulip and the daisy intertwined. 'I found it next to your rubbish bin.' He looked at her and she saw the defiant look he'd worn many times as a boy. 'I didn't think it should be thrown away.'

She looked down at the carving. Was he just talking about the picture? Her nerves tightened even more. She felt as if she were balancing on a tightrope suspended above shards of glass. She didn't want to slip in case she landed on them and got cut up even more. Didn't want to hope that maybe she'd land on marsh-mallowy pillows instead.

'It must have taken hours.'

'Sure. But then I didn't have anything else to do with my hands.'

The silence was absolute.

To cover it she lifted the lid of the box, gasping as she saw inside.

'It's for your art stuff.'

There was a removable top layer divided into several com-partments of varying sizes. Perfect for pencils, charcoals and brushes. She lifted it out by its handle. The space underneath was divided into large segments. And in each compartment lay a large block or five of Caramello.

She smiled.

'Figured you need a stash to get you through the hours you work.'

Now was the perfect opportunity. She wanted to tell him. She had a Christmas present of her own she'd been planning on offering to him. She opened her mouth and started, wanting to be on the road of no return before she lost the nerve.

'I'm leaving the hotel.'

He jerked his head up, the focus of his eyes sharpening. 'What are you going to do?'

'I'm setting up my own business.'

She read his surprise and she thought she could see concern also. So she battled on, speaking with the same defiance he had moments ago, only more urgent. 'I like numbers, Jake. I like making them work. I enjoy the accountancy. I'd never have worked so hard at it if I didn't. It wasn't all about pleasing Dad or Max. I'm not that much of a sad case.' She sighed. 'OK, that was part of it. But not all. And I love painting. So I'm not going to give either part up completely.' She paused, wondering what he'd think of her plan. He was fixed on her. 'Margaret's book is going to be published using my drawings.' She took a deep breath. 'And some of the paintings. And the plan is to release some additional products to tie in—stationery, a calendar and stuff.'

'With your paintings.'

She nodded.

'There's going to be an exhibition when the book is released.'

He looked staggered. 'That's amazing.'

She continued, not wanting the interruption until she'd explained it all. He was the first person she'd told in full. The one who mattered most. 'I'm selling the cottage and with the funds I'm going to set up a small business as a specialist accountant working for artists, writers and actors and the like—who have irregular income and have to deal with potentially tricky things like royalties and expenses. I'm just going to work on it part-time while developing my own portfolio for the exhibition.'

There. Done.

For the first time since she'd clapped eyes on him that afternoon she relaxed a little. Only one more hurdle. She waited for his response.

'How do you feel about exhibiting?'

She answered honestly. 'Terrified. But, kind of excited at the same time.' She brushed ineffectually at the yellow stains on her skirt. 'Once you knew, then Cathy at the gallery, Margaret, Lucy and Sienna, I found it wasn't so bad.'

'You've been in touch with Cathy?'

She nodded. 'You were right about her—she is great.' She took in another deep breath. 'It scares me, Jake, but if I think of it as a game it's OK. I'll do it for as long as it is fun and try not to get too uptight.' She couldn't hold the smile back as she said that. 'I've been trying to excel all my life, but I'm going to try and relax over this. Ultimately it's still for me, Jake, and there will always be paintings I paint that will only ever be for me. But I'll give it a go and if I hate it I can stop. I was halfway there anyway, doing the drawings for the book. It's just that you came along and pushed me along faster than I was willing to go.'

He looked pained. 'I'm really sorry about that, Emma. You were right; I shouldn't have. I shouldn't have sneaked in and taken the photos.'

'I know you were just trying to help. I think I would have got to this point eventually, but you just speeded up the process. And Cathy is a fabulous contact.'

'You were doing it yourself with Margaret's book.' He glanced at the box. 'Have you told your parents?'

'Not yet. I wanted...' *to tell you first* '...to be sure of a few things. I've done a painting for them for Christmas.' She stopped, conscious of his hooded stare.

'Do you have to sell the cottage? I thought you loved it.'

She shrugged. 'I'll find another place I love as much. And you were right—its location makes it a gold-mine.'

She paused, suddenly lost for words. The most important ones lodged in her throat and she couldn't quite get them out. She felt the chasm between them and didn't know how to bridge it. She waited, wanting some sign of encouragement but unable to see it.

'That's really great, Emma.'

She couldn't read his expression. His words sounded so final, so 'end of conversation'. Not interested, then. It *had* just been about helping her out—and a fling on the side.

'Thank you very much for the box—it's beautiful.' Stilted, stammering, she turned to head home, staring at defeat and despair.

It seemed as if he was about to let her leave, but suddenly blurted out a question. 'You didn't get the flowers I sent you?'

She turned back immediately. 'No. I was away.'

Heavy-lidded, he watched her relentlessly.

She tried to ask as nonchalantly as she could. 'What were they?'

'Gardenias.'

She'd drawn them only recently and had written the meaning in her neat script beneath. Painted them only the last weekend and destroyed the result because she'd felt such a fool.

I love you in secret.

Did he know that was their hidden message? She was shaking from the inside out. 'Why gardenias?'

She'd never seen him so tense. And then he sighed and the words seemed to come from deep inside. 'You said everyone has secrets, Emma.' He breathed in and as he exhaled his tumbled out. 'I love you. That's my secret. I love you and I always will.'

CHAPTER FIFTEEN

'YOU'RE kidding.' Emma was so stunned she couldn't stop the rudeness of her question.

She watched as for once Jake's was the face to colour. 'Actually for once in my life I'm not joking.'

She glanced up to the ceiling thinking that the roar she could hear was some freak hailstorm. No, it was just her pulse crazily loud, irregular and fast.

He was talking again, just as fast as her heartbeat and she strained to hear every word. 'I'm sorry, Emma. I'm sorry I started this out as just a fling; I'm sorry I took photos of your paintings; I'm sorry I broke your trust.'

'You didn't break my trust, Jake. I've always trusted you. And I know you thought you were doing me a favour.'

'I just wanted to help you because I thought I could and because I wanted you to be happy.'

'Because you care.' Statement not question. But she still couldn't believe the way in which he cared.

'I care. A lot. More than a lot. But I don't care what you do, how much you earn, how successful or otherwise you might be. I'll still love you. I'll still be here for you. I'll still support you no matter what. It's you I love, Emma, you for being you. You don't have to do anything other than be yourself for me. And I know that wanting to please people, wanting to achieve things for them is part of you, but you don't need to do that for me. OK?' He took a breath and continued. 'I don't want you showing your paintings if you don't want to—not because I thought you should or Cathy or Margaret or anyone else. You should only do it if you want to.'

'It is because I want to, Jake. I do. It started as a secret because I was scared of what Dad would say—as a kid, his approval meant everything. Then the fact it was secret became habit. And I felt that people would expect the best from me. I became scared that if I didn't live up to that I'd be rejected. Stupid, huh?'

'No.' A faint smile touched his face. 'I'm glad you held it to yourself for so long. I'm glad it was me that you shared it with.'

She wasn't at all sure they were still talking about her painting.

'So what do you say, Emma? Fancy...' He paused, his tension audible to both of them. He tried again. 'Fancy spending a little more time with me, go on a few dates. Give me a chance?'

'You don't need a chance.' She couldn't lift her voice higher than a whisper and he moved closer to hear her. Not close enough. Her body and soul were screaming out to touch him but she couldn't get the words out of her damn mouth. 'Jake...' She moved towards him.

His face lit up.

'Jake?' Sienna's voice rang out, and she appeared in the doorway of the garage a split-second later. 'Jake, I need you to lift the crate of...'

Emma pulled back, sweeping her raised hand through her own hair instead of reaching for Jake as she'd intended.

'You're going to have to do it yourself, Sienna. I'm busy right now.' Emma had never heard such an abrupt tone from him. Certainly never when talking to Sienna. He grabbed Emma's hand and led her out to the staircase

Emma turned her head to see Sienna standing, mouth open, staring after them. Hot colour flooded into her cheeks as Sienna's burst of laugher rang in her ears.

She matched him step for step as he bounded up the stairs. He let her hand go as he opened the door and she walked ahead into the middle of the room, looking about, but supremely conscious of him shutting and locking the door. Superficially she took in the divan against the wall, the beer fridge, kettle and toaster. An ancient stereo system sat on the ground with a box overflowing with CDs next to it.

The magic of the previous moment had gone and she was so thrown she didn't know if she'd dreamt it. She covered her confusion with a little laugh. 'This is your "man cave".'

His fingers roughed his hair. 'Yeah, I guess. Once I started working I used to sleep here sometimes—if I was home late and didn't want to wake the others in the house.'

'Did you do a lot of entertaining here?' She couldn't help asking.

He flashed a grin. 'Not nearly as much as you think.' She threw him a sceptical look.

'Really. I was talking it up earlier.'

'And now you're talking it down to make me feel better.'

He fixed on her. 'Does it bother you?'

'I'm human, of *course* it bothers me.'

'Good, because the thought of you with someone else makes me so mad I could just…' He stopped and laughed.

'But I'm so not your type!' She quickly walked away, wincing at her needy outburst. The window she stood at looked down on Jake's pool and over the fence to her parents' backyard—the manicured lawn and formal flower beds, the marquee set up for the annual bash.

He followed her, stopped to stand right behind her and her excitement level ratcheted up a notch. *Soon.* But they needed to talk. They hadn't been talking nearly enough and that was part of the problem.

'There is no "type" for me, Emma. There is only you.' He turned her towards him. 'Until now, I could take or leave my girlfriends. Fun. Good friends, even. But nothing that serious. It's so different with you. I can't leave you, Emma. I can't ever leave you. You *make* my life.'

She stared into his eyes, saw the honesty shining out and told him her own secret. 'I had such a crush on you.'

'No-o-o.' His hands dropped to his sides.

'Uh-huh.' She laughed at his shocked expression. It emboldened her to be completely blunt. 'For *years*. Ever since that day in the park when you were so nice to me.'

'Nice?' He stared, lost in the memory. 'I put my arm around you to give you a hug like I would Sienna and suddenly I was on fire. I should have known then that there was something special about you. About us.' His chest rose and fell as he took a deep breath. 'You were into me?'

'I've always been into you. So cool, so funny, so good-looking. You listened to me, Jake. No one had listened to me like that.'

'Yeah, but I stopped, didn't I? I stopped listening right when I should have been paying the most attention.'

'You were just wanting to help me. I know that. And you were right. Sharing things is fun. Sharing things with the people you care about is fun.'

'I like sharing things with you, Emma.'

She smiled, the sauce bubbling forth. 'I like sharing me with you, Jake.' She batted her lashes.

He chuckled and his hands were on her arms again, still rubbing, but drawing her closer, millimetre by millimetre until she was close enough for him to rest his forehead on hers. 'I've been thinking of you every moment, Emma. Waking, sleeping. Thinking of you.' He sighed and lifted his head, looking into her eyes with such a sweet intensity and she felt a crazy calm over her, despite the desire burning inside. It was all going to be OK. 'I saw you standing in front of me in that bar and you're all grown-up and we're out of this town and you had this look in your eye and I thought, Why not? A fun moment with someone a little different.'

Confidence sent the blood flowing in her veins. 'But it wasn't.'

'Nuh-uh.' He shook his head and stroked the tip of his finger across her lips. 'That one kiss wasn't nearly enough. Especially when I found out it was only for show. I wanted all of you all to myself.'

She chased the path of his finger with her tongue and as a reward he stepped even closer.

'I figured I could get close to you, at least fool around just a little. I thought the more I touched, the less I'd want to.' He grunted. 'Wrong. Totally wrong.'

She took the final step closer, bringing them into complete contact. 'You set up our game.'

His face split into that gorgeous grin that he got when he was having wicked thoughts. 'Good idea, wasn't it? Play at being lovers. But it backfired.'

She raised an eyebrow.

'I couldn't control it, could I? For me it got very serious, very quickly and I knew I was in big trouble.' He looked apologetic. 'I wasn't planning on serious, Emma. I thought it would burn out. But instead all I wanted was to be with you. I wanted to make you happy. And I thought I could help arrange that.' His eyes narrowed in his frown.

'Being happy isn't something you can control for me, Jake. That's something I have to take care of myself. And I'm working on it. I've redirected my career. I've opened up about my painting. There was only one thing I had yet to do.'

'What's that?'

'I'm going to Auckland. Ticket's booked for next week.'

She felt his stillness. 'What are you going there for?'

'You.' She took his face in her hands. 'I wanted more of you. Was coming on the chance you might want more too.' She shrugged sheepishly.

'Sure.' He slid his hands down her back. 'I want more.'

She slid her hands through his hair, curling her fingers into the thick locks. 'No more games, then?'

'The only game I'm planning on playing in the future is Scrabble.'

'*Scrabble?*' She laughed, tilting her chin at him. 'Jake, you are a closet geek.'

'Yeah, well, you're a closet saucy minx so I guess that makes us even.'

She let the minx out of the bag. 'You're still going to play with me, though, aren't you?'

He lifted the hem of her tee shirt and stroked his palms down her bare skin, pressing her against him. She practically purred as he unzipped her skirt.

'I've just rolled the dice.'

Their eyes met. Every cell in her body in tune, ready. It was the moment she'd been waiting for since she'd seen him on her father's deck.

Finally he lowered his mouth to her upturned one.

Ignition.

He kissed her. She kissed him. Beautiful, rejoicing, tender, and she revelled in his touch. He stroked, smoothed, and slid his fingers, hands and body over her skin.

And he was going too damn slow.

'Jake, please hurry.'

'Why, you got somewhere to be? You got a plane to catch?'

She choked, the gurgle of laughter caught on a sob of desire.

He kissed her, and kissed her again. 'It's all going to happen, honey.'

But it still wasn't enough and the only way to get it was to steal the march. Catching him by surprise, she pushed him onto the divan, stripping him of his tee shirt—at least managing to get it over his head and down as far as his elbows as he lifted his arms up high for her.

'I want you, Jake Rendel.' She kissed him, bruising her lips as she passionately pressed them against his hard muscles. Moving over his chest and up his neck to his jaw. 'Get undressed, dammit.'

Her urgency was infectious. He shrugged his arms free of the tee, lifted her so he could ditch his jeans as fast as was humanly possible. Then he leaned over her, his body pressing length to length. She couldn't think of anything else. Nothing mattered any more. All she wanted was him, in her, all the way. *Right now.*

'Do me, Jake.' She arched up to him, half begging, half teasing. '*Do* me.'

Wicked delight radiated from him. 'Emma, I'm not going to make it if you talk like that.'

'I'm not afraid to ask for what I want any more, Jake. And I want you.'

She pushed up, inviting him, and he took his place with a fierce thrust.

'You've got me.'

And then the dynamic changed completely—frivolity vanishing. She cried out, long and loud as he filled her. He'd plunged deep only a couple of times when it hit, the rapturous waves beating over her. She swept her arms down him as her body locked in ecstasy, screamed out the pleasure. It was the fastest road to orgasm she'd ever been on. She panted, but wasn't given the chance to recover as he kept up the stroke, building her up again. She opened her eyes to watch his answer.

But he didn't come with her. Instead he continued to hold back, working to rouse her again, intensely focussed on her, all traces of humour gone. 'Everything is so raw when I'm with you. You leave my heart so vulnerable. It scares me.'

'Jake.' She knew he heard the love in her voice and then she told him anyway as the sensations crested. 'I love you.'

'Say it again.'

She did and he closed his eyes, opening them again to reveal painful honesty. 'This feels so right. I never thought anything would be right again.'

'It's OK, Jake.'

'I really thought I'd lost you.'

She wrapped her arms around him and hugged him tight to her. 'You could never lose me. I've always been here. We just didn't know it.' And she moved with him, started to drive him, made it faster, harder, whispering to him, voicing her excitement and exciting him with it. But still he held back, his body an instrument of pleasure for her. It wasn't until she'd buckled yet again that he finally spent his love into her.

'Do me a favour.'

'Mmm.' Deliriously happy, giddy from multiple orgasms, curled in his arms, she couldn't move.

'Whatever I ask, you have to say yes.'

She smiled. 'I am not having a threesome.'

'Just say yes, Emma. It's not hard.'

She reached behind her. 'Yes, it is.'

'I'm not kidding.' The tension in his voice caught her. She heard his drawn breath. 'Just say yes.'

She turned her head and looked at him. 'You're serious.' She saw his unsmiling face, unusually strained. 'Jake?'

'Marry me.'

She blinked, the buzz in her ears blocking her comprehension. She whispered. 'I'm sorry, I'm going to have to get you to say that again.'

'Marry me. Please.'

She blinked again. And again—rapidly as the stinging sheen of tears hampered her vision. One spilt over and his hands came to frame her face.

'I really need to hear it, Em.'

She took in a shaky breath and mentally debated her answer. 'Sure.' She managed to say it smoothly and then beamed at him through the twin rivers tripping down her cheeks. '*Yes*. I sure will marry you.'

He shouted and wrapped his arms around her, rolling over and taking her with him so she lay on top of him. Her tears spilt onto his chest.

'No more.' He kissed them away from her eyes. 'No more.'

She buried her face in his neck, breathing in his warm masculinity—the faint stubble of his jaw pressing on her forehead. She'd never imagined such happiness and she shut her eyes fast in case it was a dream—she never wanted to wake from it.

His hand left her back and she felt him reaching for something.

'Emma.'

She had to open her eyes then. He'd pulled a box out of the pocket of his jeans.

'I was going to put it in your art box but I chickened out.' He handed it to her, his expression solemn.

A ring box. Her eyes widened. 'Jake.' Propped up on her elbows, her naked body flowing over his—it wasn't how she'd ever imagined she'd receive a wedding proposal, much less an engagement ring. Her heart thundered as she lifted the lid. Her eyes widened more.

'This is, um…' She stared at the contents. A chunky plastic flower ring, the kind you'd get in the two-dollar store for a four-year-old niece. Bright yellow with white petals on a garish blue circle. Adjustable size and everything. She looked up to see him grinning broadly. He winked.

'I want you to come with me to choose your proper ring— you know, we decide things *together* from now on. But I wanted to have something for the moment.'

He took it out of the box and she held out her hand, laughter lighting between them. 'You want me on my knees?'

'Of course. I want you every which way.'

He snorted as he slid the toy ring down her finger. 'Good thing you have such small hands.'

'Where'd you get it? Christmas cracker?'

He pretended to look wounded.

She fluttered her fingers, admiringly. 'I'll treasure it for ever.' She started to giggle.

'What's so funny?'

'Can you imagine Sienna and Lucy as bridesmaids?'

'Hell.' He shuddered. 'You don't think we should elope?'

'What? And deny your mum the pleasure of seeing her fine son get married? I'd never do it to her. Besides, I want the meringue.' She wrinkled her nose. 'I'm going to have to wear fake tan.'

'Honey, you could wear a sack and you'll still look beautiful to me.'

She cracked up. 'Oh, Jake, you smooth talker.' She ruffled his hair and planted a kiss on the underside of his chin. 'I am going to like being married to you.'

He tipped his head down and suavely replied. 'And I'm going to love being married to you.'

Their smiles melted in the kiss and she felt the flick of fire again, but on hearing the car doors slamming on the street below she lifted her head. 'I'm going to have to go.' The party would be warming up and she needed to be there, taking her place as the dutiful daughter.

'You don't think you're going without me, do you?'

'You never come to this party.'

'As far as I'm concerned it's our engagement party. I'm coming. Besides, your old man isn't that bad.'

They pulled their clothes back on, hindered by the lingering kisses in between each item, the slide of his body into hers.

As they dressed for the second time a question occurred to her. 'What were you going to do if I wasn't here?'

'Send you the art box by courier and hope you saw the message.'

'The picture?'

He shook his head. 'There's a less subtle message carved on the bottom.'

'What is it?'

He just grinned. She flew down the stairs to where the box still sat on the bench in the garage. She tipped it upside down to see underneath and softened in delight. She leaned back, knowing he would be behind her. She lifted her arm around his neck as he nuzzled hers.

Happiness, relief and plain old-fashioned lust glowed.

The box sat, forgotten for the moment, with the little carving in the top left hand corner showing for all the world to see:

J.R. ♥ E.D.

HARLEQUIN *Presents*

**Harlequin Presents brings you
a brand-new duet by star author**

Sharon Kendrick

THE GREEK BILLIONAIRES' BRIDES

Possessed by two Greek billionaire brothers

Alexandros Pavlidis always ended his affairs before
boredom struck. After a passionate relationship with
Rebecca Gibbs, he never expected to see her again.
Until she arrived at his office—pregnant, with twins!

Don't miss

THE GREEK TYCOON'S CONVENIENT WIFE,

on sale July 2008

THE BOSS'S MISTRESS

Out of the office...and into his bed

These ruthless, powerful men are used
to having their own way in the office—
and with their mistresses they're also
boss in the bedroom!

**Don't miss any of our fantastic stories
in the July 2008 collection:**

**#13 THE ITALIAN
TYCOON'S MISTRESS**
by CATHY WILLIAMS

#14 RUTHLESS BOSS, HIRED WIFE
by KATE HEWITT

#15 IN THE TYCOON'S BED
by KATHRYN ROSS

**#16 THE RICH MAN'S
RELUCTANT MISTRESS**
by MARGARET MAYO

REQUEST YOUR FREE BOOKS!

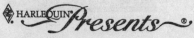 HARLEQUIN® *Presents*®

PASSION GUARANTEED SEDUCTION

2 FREE NOVELS PLUS 2
FREE GIFTS!

YES! Please send me 2 FREE Harlequin Presents® novels and my 2 FREE gifts (gifts are worth about $10). After receiving them, if I don't wish to receive any more books, I can return the shipping statement marked "cancel". If I don't cancel, I will receive 6 brand-new novels every month and be billed just $4.05 per book in the U.S. or $4.74 per book in Canada, plus 25¢ shipping and handling per book and applicable taxes, if any*. That's a savings of close to 15% off the cover price! I understand that accepting the 2 free books and gifts places me under no obligation to buy anything. I can always return a shipment and cancel at any time. Even if I never buy another book, the two free books and gifts are mine to keep forever.

106 HDN ERRW 306 HDN ERRL

Name	(PLEASE PRINT)
Address	Apt. #
City	State/Prov. Zip/Postal Code

Signature (if under 18, a parent or guardian must sign)

Mail to the Harlequin Reader Service:
IN U.S.A.: P.O. Box 1867, Buffalo, NY 14240-1867
IN CANADA: P.O. Box 609, Fort Erie, Ontario L2A 5X3

Not valid to current subscribers of Harlequin Presents books.

Want to try two free books from another line?
Call 1-800-873-8635 or visit www.morefreebooks.com.

* Terms and prices subject to change without notice. N.Y. residents add applicable sales tax. Canadian residents will be charged applicable provincial taxes and GST. This offer is limited to one order per household. All orders subject to approval. Credit or debit balances in a customer's account(s) may be offset by any other outstanding balance owed by or to the customer. Please allow 4 to 6 weeks for delivery. Offer available while quantities last.

Your Privacy: Harlequin Books is committed to protecting your privacy. Our Privacy Policy is available online at www.eHarlequin.com or upon request from the Reader Service. From time to time we make our lists of customers available to reputable third parties who may have a product or service of interest to you. If you would prefer we not share your name and address, please check here. ☐

HP08

I ♥ HARLEQUIN *Presents*

BROUGHT TO YOU BY FANS OF HARLEQUIN PRESENTS.

We are its editors and authors
and biggest fans—and we'd
love to hear from YOU!

Subscribe today to our online blog at
www.iheartpresents.com